'Come on, Jill. It's time for Christmas.'

'Coming.' Jill stuffed a last, crunchy piece of bacon into her mouth. She was still chewing it as she picked up the bag of gifts that she had hurriedly put together yesterday.

Jack followed, camera still in hand.

'Ho, ho, ho! Sorry I'm a bit late,' Santa boomed. 'Ballochburn is a bit out of the way, you know.'

The children excitedly tore into parcels. The Friends of the Hospital had done themselves proud, and there were plenty of new gifts of toys and clothing.

There would be no chance to talk to Jill about anything personal at the hospital, Jack thought, and he felt disheartened. Until Jill looked at him. Caught his gaze properly for the first time that day. And smil

That warm, lovin good at.

Just for him.

No. This was it.

Fate had dropped him from the sky because the answer had been waiting for him, right here in the heart of stone fruit country. And he had found it.

Dear Reader

Christmas. It's one of those words that conjures up so many images, isn't it?

A celebration of love symbolised by gifts between lovers, friends, families, and even whole communities. It doesn't matter whether it's cold and snowy, like most Christmas cards depict, or hot and sunny as it usually is here in the southern hemisphere. The traditions are more similar than different, and the spirit is always the same.

The chaos of the Christmas season is the same as well. There's too much to do and an obligation to feel happy that, for some people, can just accentuate the feeling of being left out. For them, Christmas can be a poignant reminder of what is missing in their lives. I chose a setting for this story that brings back happy memories of an area where I spent many summer holidays as a child, and my intention was to try and capture some Christmas magic amongst the seasonal chaos.

My hero, Jack, is one of those people who can't enjoy Christmas. He has nothing to give so he has no intention of accepting anything—even when he meets someone prepared to give him everything.

Magic was definitely needed. I hope you find it in their story, and in your own celebration of Christmas this year.

Happy reading

With love

Alison

CHRISTMAS BRIDE-TO-BE

BY
ALISON ROBERTS

MILLS & BOON
Pure reading pleasure

First published in Great Britain 2007
Harlequin Mills & Boon Limited,
Eton House, 18-24 Paradise Road, Richmond, Surrey TW9 1SR

© Alison Roberts 2007

ISBN: 978 0 263 85274 5

Set in Times Roman 10½ on 12¾ pt
03-1107-47160

Printed and bound in Spain
by Litografia Rosés, S.A., Barcelona

Alison Roberts lives in Christchurch, New Zealand. She began her working career as a primary school teacher, but now juggles available working hours between writing and active duty as an ambulance officer. Throwing in a large dose of parenting, housework, gardening and pet-minding keeps life busy, and teenage daughter Becky is responsible for an increasing number of days spent on equestrian pursuits. Finding time for everything can be a challenge, but the rewards make the effort more than worthwhile.

Recent titles by the same author:

THE PLAYBOY DOCTOR'S PROPOSAL†
THE ITALIAN DOCTOR'S PERFECT FAMILY
   (Mediterranean Doctors)
A FATHER BEYOND COMPARE*
ONE NIGHT TO WED*
EMERGENCY BABY*
THE SURGEON'S PERFECT MATCH
THE DOCTOR'S UNEXPECTED PROPOSAL†

Specialist Emergency Rescue Team
†Crocodile Creek*

For Carol, who's not a Christmas baby
but is still very special. With love

CHAPTER ONE

THE sound was threatening.

A low growl that made the hairs on the back of Jillian Metcalf's neck stand on end.

She froze, the sealed sharps container she was about to deposit in the designated bin suspended in mid-air.

The sound took her straight back to those horror movies she and her friends had loved to be terrified by. Way back, when they had been too young to be allowed too much freedom and the only Friday night entertainment had been a video at one of their houses. They had sat in the dark, clutching each other and shrieking…like when the werewolf had been just about to launch a gruesome attack.

Just after it had growled.

Cursing her overactive imagination, Jill straightened her spine, albeit cautiously. Werewolves did not hide out behind the rubbish bins of a small rural hospital. And they weren't known for surprise attacks in the blazing midday sun.

Tilting sideways so that she could see between the tall green recycling bins beside the large skip, Jill pushed back the blonde curls that the breeze was playing with and peered into the shadows. The gleam of bared white fangs accompanied by another growl might have continued to seem threatening but as her eyes made the adjustment from the glare of the white pebbles paving this courtyard area to the gloom of the shade, Jill could see the eyes of the wolf.

Sad eyes.

She put down the yellow plastic sharps bin and dropped to a crouch.

'Hey,' she said softly. 'What's the matter, girl? Are you hurt?'

The growling stopped, replaced by rapid panting. It didn't matter that Jill was a doctor and not a vet. She knew the animal was breathing too fast. She watched as the bared teeth disappeared and a long pink tongue hung out.

'You're hot and thirsty,' she informed the dog. 'And no wonder! I'm not surprised you've tried to find some shade. Want to come out and find a drink instead?'

The answer seemed to be in the negative. Jill eyed the gap between the bins. It had never bothered her unduly that she had the solid build of a country girl but there was no way she could fit in that gap. She could wheel all the recycling bins out of the way but they would be heavy and it was a very hot day. Unless it was too injured, it would be much easier to coax the dog to come out.

'Don't go away,' Jill advised. 'I'll be right back.'

It was a quick trip to the back door of Ballochburn Hospital's kitchens.

'I need a bowl,' Jill announced.

A large woman banged the door of an oven shut and then peeled a teatowel from where it had been looped through her apron string. She mopped a very red face.

'Where are your manners, Jilly Metcalf?'

Jill had to bite her lip to kill the grin. Never mind that she was temporarily in the position of being one of the doctors in charge of this hospital and technically Maisie Drummond's boss. She may as well have been ten years old again and stealing gooseberries from the back of the Drummonds' orchard.

'Please?' she added obligingly.

Maisie sniffed thoughtfully but Jill knew better than to appear impatient. The portable radio on the window-sill filled the silence with the New Zealand version of 'The Twelve Days of Christmas'.

'And a pukeko in a ponga tree…'

'And what would you be needing a bowl for?' As expected, Maisie had made her decision in Jill's favour. 'I thought you'd finished your ward rounds.'

'There's a dog,' Jill explained. 'Hiding behind the bins. I think it might be hurt and it's too scared to come out. And it's thirsty,' she added firmly. 'It needs water.'

'I'm not surprised,' Maisie muttered, mopping her face again. 'Must be over thirty degrees out there.'

'Hotter in here,' Jill said sympathetically. 'There's a nice breeze outside, though. Why don't you open some windows?'

Maisie muttered something almost inaudible about it being a totally inadequate form of air-conditioning and that nobody else would put up with her working conditions, but she moved to pull up one of the heavy wooden sash windows. The cord had clearly been broken long enough for the positioning of a brick to keep it open to be automatic. The breeze had picked up and both women turned their faces towards the welcome cooler air.

'A bowl, you said?'

'Yes, please, Maisie.'

'For a dog.'

'Yes.'

'Whose dog?'

'I have no idea.'

'This is a hospital, Jilly, not a veterinary clinic.'

'I know that. I'll take it home until I can find its owner.'

'It's unhygienic,' Maisie grumbled as she opened a cupboard. 'You can't go using people bowls on dogs. Not in a hospital.'

'I'll put it in the steriliser.'

'You'd better.' Maisie turned on a tap over one of the vast stainless-steel sinks and filled the bowl with cold water.

Jill skirted a trolley set out with lunch-trays. Beautiful trays with sandwiches and Maisie's famous home-made chocolate cake and peeled slices of fruit. The trays all had names on them and Jill could see the one labelled for old Mrs Hinkley. The sandwiches were full of egg and parsley. The crusts had been removed and the slivers of fruit were thin enough to eat even if she was refusing to put her teeth in again.

How many hospitals in the world would there be where patients got this kind of individual attention? Mind you, how many hospitals only had four or five inpatients and too many eerie rooms containing empty beds and had managed to survive this long without being shut down?

It was probably the last of its kind and it would be a sad day when it disappeared like all the others.

Jill pushed the thought away somewhat guiltily. It was partly her fault that it might eventually close. Finding doctors to live and work in rural areas was increasingly difficult and she herself was a prime example of one of the new generation of doctors who preferred to work in a large city with services that covered after-hours care and the immediate back-up of the specialist skills and resources a large hospital could provide.

She held out her hands to take the bowl of water but Maisie didn't hand it over.

'I'm coming, too,' the older woman said.

'There's no need. You're busy—it must be time to deliver the lunches.'

'I've been doing this job for thirty years, young lady. I was doing it the day you got born upstairs and I'll still be doing it when you swan off to Australia and that exciting new job you've got lined up. Don't you go telling me how I should be doing *my* job.'

'Sorry.' Jill had no desire to step on any toes and she certainly didn't want to spend the time listening to one of Maisie's prolonged lectures. The poor dog outside had already been waiting too long for a drink. She turned towards the back door. 'It's just out here.'

'I do know where the bins are.' Maisie stomped along behind Jill. 'I'm just coming to make sure it hasn't made too much of a mess. And that it doesn't have rabies.'

'We don't have rabies in New Zealand, Maisie.'

'Always a first time,' Maisie warned. 'You sure it's not just a big possum? They carry tuberculosis, you know.'

'It's definitely a dog.'

A very hot, frightened dog. Jill pushed the bowl well down into the space between the bins.

'There you go, girl,' she said soothingly. 'Nice cold water.'

The dog didn't move.

'Don't worry,' Jill added. 'Nobody's going to hurt you.' Her voice was soft, almost a croon. 'It's just water. Nice and cold. Because you're thirsty and hot, aren't you, sweetie?'

A snort came from Maisie's direction. 'You've always been barmy about animals, you have. Always dragging home some poor hedgehog or bird or anything else that couldn't get away from you. Drove your poor mum and dad up the wall, you did.'

'Did I?' Jill turned to raise her eyebrows at Maisie. 'They never *seemed* to mind.'

From the corner of her eye, she could see the dog taking advantage of the lack of direct attention. It slunk forward on its belly. Seconds later they heard the sound of vigorous lapping and Jill beamed.

'Good *girl*,' she said approvingly. 'Are you going to come out now and let us have a proper look at you?'

'It's probably a boy,' Maisie said. 'And it'll probably bite you.'

'No-o-o.' Jill poked her hand into the gap and let the dog sniff the backs of her fingers. 'You wouldn't do that, would you, darling?' She could see the faint movement of a shaggy tail. An apologetic sort of wag. 'I think it's hungry, Maisie.'

'I'm not cooking lunch for a dog and that's *that*.' Maisie folded her arms.

'Come on, girl.' Jill scratched an ear hiding in matted, shaggy hair and then moved backwards. 'Out you come.'

It came. With its tail firmly between its legs and a drooping head, but it moved out of its hiding place to slink closer to Jill.

'It's not wearing a collar. I reckon it's lost.'

'Dumped, more likely. And no wonder!' Maisie stared at the dog. 'That's the ugliest mutt I've seen in all my born days. What *is* it?'

'Might be a farm dog. There's a bit of bearded collie in there, I would think, to give it such long hair.' Jill grinned as she eyed the tawny tufts of hair that sprouted in all directions. 'You're just having a bad hair day, aren't you, sweets?'

'Got spaniel eyes, if you ask me,' Maisie pronounced. 'Pathetic-looking thing, isn't it?'

'It's so thin.' Jill chewed her bottom lip. 'I can feel all its ribs.'

Maisie sighed wearily. 'I'll see if there's a few scraps in the fridge.'

'And it's…' Jill was running her hands gently over the matted coat. 'Oh, boy!'

'What?'

'I think it's pregnant. The tummy sure doesn't match the state of the ribs.'

'That'll be why it got dumped, then.' Maisie tutted her disapproval. 'People can't be bothered paying for kennels when they want to go on their Christmas holidays, and if they *can* be bothered, I'll bet kennels won't even take dogs that are about to whelp.'

'Well, there's room at *this* inn.' Jill stepped away and patted her leg. 'Can you walk, sweetie? I'll take you home. It's not far.'

The dog needed no encouragement. It moved in order to stay in contact with Jill's leg.

'I won't be long,' Jill told Maisie. 'I was planning to drop home and have lunch with the folks, anyway. I'll be back to do the clinic at one and tell Ange I've got my pager on if she wants me for anything on the wards.'

Maisie waved her off. 'Don't forget to wash your hands. You don't know what you might catch from that mutt.'

It wasn't a long journey.

There was an apartment within the old hospital complex for a resident doctor, but thirty-five years ago the newly married Dr James Metcalf had purchased an old villa adjacent to the hospital grounds. The hinges of the gate he'd put in the back fence had almost rusted through but it was still used often enough to keep it serviceable and the track that led beneath the century-old oak trees and through the carpet of bluebells in springtime was so well worn it would probably be there for ever.

The dog cringed at the loud creak of the rusty hinges and Jill stooped to pet the animal.

'You're safe now,' she said. 'It's OK, honest!'

The swing at the bottom of the garden was surrounded by apple trees laden with half-formed fruit. A cacophony of cicadas sang about summer and the only weeding being done in the oversized and neglected vegetable patch was courtesy of several black and white spotted Wyandotte hens.

'Rule number one,' Jill warned the dog, 'don't eat the hens.'

A hugely fat ginger cat eyed the newcomer warily from its position in the sun at the top of the steps.

'Rule number two,' Jill whispered, 'be nice to Marmalade.'

The screen door leading into the kitchen banged shut as it always had.

'Hi, Mum!' Jill called. 'I'm starving! What's for lunch?'

The silence was unexpected but not worrying. As the wife of a small community's only long-term doctor, Hope Metcalf was involved enough to keep her very busy, especially this close to Christmas. She was probably caught up in a choir practice or helping to set up for pets' day at the local primary school or she could just be working out the front in the riotous cottage garden that was her pride and joy.

There was no sign of Jill's father either, but he'd had a few house calls to make that morning and, given the area the practice had to cover, it could have taken a long time.

'Never mind,' Jill told the dog. 'I'll make myself a sandwich. Wait till you taste Mum's ham. It's fabulous.'

Ears that had been as droopy as the tail pricked up. Liquid brown eyes fastened on Jill with an expression that squeezed her heart. She bent down and patted the dog again.

'You're a darling, aren't you? I'm sure you haven't really been abandoned. Who would do something like that?'

She sighed unconsciously as she straightened. It wasn't that she was out of touch with the reality of what went on in the world, it was just that bad things seemed to have a sharper focus here.

This community, this house, her family were Jill's rock. The solid foundation her life had been built on. Familiar, pre-dictable…*safe*. A haven she carried with her even when she was a thousand miles away in Auckland. She'd missed it des-perately two years ago when her marriage had crumbled.

Yes, she had made a mistake. But she knew she wasn't mistaken in believing that the kind of relationship she wanted *did* exist. That it was possible she could still find it…one day. She'd just be more careful next time. Look a lot harder before she leapt.

The timing of this, her first long visit to thè trusted reality of home since she'd left to go to medical school, couldn't have been better, given that her final divorce papers had arrived in the mail the very day she had been packing to leave on her way to a new life. She'd actually been finally able to pull off that wedding band. To leave it behind.

Even the mess on the scrubbed Kauri table in this huge kitchen was comfortingly familiar. A whole week's worth of newspapers neatly folded and stacked. Bills that needed at-tention. A sugar bowl and salt pig made of crude clay coils that had been Jill's own creations in pottery class at primary school when she had been ten years old. Never mind that they wobbled and the glaze had been patchy. Mum said they were rustic and she loved them and they'd been on the table for nearly twenty years now.

The mess on the faded pink Formica bench was a lot less comforting. If there was one thing her mother hated, it was a dirty bench. She would never leave the house with her workspace looking like that unless…

Unless something disturbingly out of the ordinary had occurred.

The bang of the screen door was a relief, until Jill turned to find it was her father entering the kitchen.

'Where's Mum?'

'Isn't she here?'

'No.'

Jim Metcalf frowned. 'But she knows what time clinic starts. I've only got half an hour for lunch.'

'She must have gone somewhere in a hurry. It's not like her to leave dishes not done.'

Jim's gaze raked the cluttered bench but then dropped. 'Good Lord, what's *that*?'

'A dog.' Jill bent to provide a reassuring scratch for the head pressed anxiously against her knee. 'A stray dog.'

'Looks like a doormat on legs. Put it outside.'

The grumpy tone was familiar enough to ignore. 'Mum didn't say anything about having to go out early. I wonder why she didn't leave a note? I hope Aunty Faith isn't sick or something.'

'Doubt it. If I'm half as healthy as she is when I'm ninety-three I'll be more than happy.' Jim was still staring at the dog.

'That animal stinks. What *is* it with bringing home waifs and strays? You're just like your mother.'

Jill was taken aback by the edge of vehemence in his tone. Had Maisie been right? Had she driven her parents mad with the various animals she had 'rescued' all those years ago?

'I'll give it a bath,' she offered.

Jim grunted. 'I suppose you've already given it a name.'

'No.' Jill smiled with relief. She had only imagined the air of real grievance. It had always been the stamp of her father's acquiescence, if not approval, to bestow a name on any new additions to the family. 'Any suggestions?'

'Fly. It's bound to attract a few, smelling like that.'

'She won't smell when she's had a bath.' Jill looked down at her feet. 'I think she's beautiful. I might call her Bella.'

Her father's expression suggested she was as barmy as Maisie had accused her of being, but whatever he was about to say was cut off by a strident beeping.

'It's me,' Jill said unnecessarily.

'Must be a PRIME page, then.'

Jill was the only one of the two doctors wearing a second paging device. With rural ambulance services manned by well-trained but voluntary crews, providing medical back-up for emergency callouts was just another part of a country doctor's workload. Having come straight from a run of working in a large emergency department, Dr Metcalf senior had handed Jill the pager on her first day as his temporary locum.

'You're far more qualified to wear this than I am,' he'd said. 'The Jeep's got a full kit in the back.'

Jill went straight to the wall phone at one end of the kitchen bench. She scribbled information on a piece of paper and hung up within a minute.

'There's been a light plane crash,' she told her father. 'It was aiming for the airfield but came down a few paddocks early on Bruce Mandeville's farm. Only one occupant but he's unconscious.'

'You'd better get your skates on, then.'

'It's miles away. The ambulance is out on a long-distance transfer and it'll take awhile to get the other truck on the road.' To find crew for the old back-up vehicle in Ballochburn's emergency vehicle fleet could mean pulling people in from fruit-picking or sheep-shearing duties. 'I'll be late for the clinic.'

'I'll do the clinic.'

'You sure?' Jill was already heading for the door. She barely noticed the dog shadowing her every move.

'Of course I'm sure.' Her father sounded remarkably like Maisie had a little earlier. 'How the hell do you think I've been managing for the last six months?'

'Sorry.' Jill pulled open the screen door. 'I'll see you later, then.'

Was she still missing something here? A level of tension that was causing the people she loved the most to snap and snarl at each other?

Or was she overreacting? Allowing the new tension that this emergency call had created to infect everything else happening around her?

Jill opened the door of the Jeep. She stuck the magnetic light on the roof and plugged its cord into the cigarette lighter inside. It would start flashing bright orange as soon as she turned the vehicle on. Nobody would ticket her for exceeding the speed limit.

About to jump into the driver's seat, Jill noticed the dog.

Just sitting. Clearly expecting to be abandoned again. There was no time to find a safe place to leave it.

'Hop in, Bella,' Jill ordered. 'We're going for a ride in a fast car.'

CHAPTER TWO

He was conscious now.

Jill could see the man sitting in the long, dry grass on the side of a slope, his shoulders hunched, his head in his hands. A very dejected picture.

And no wonder!

Below him—upside down—was a small, gleamingly new-looking, two-seater aircraft with a seriously bent propeller.

Bruce Mandeville was standing beside the plane, rubbing the back of his sunburnt neck. Three black and white dogs lay at his feet, tongues lolling. Bella, who had been looking out the window of the Jeep, saw the farm dogs and slid down to cringe on the floor behind the two front seats as Jill brought the vehicle to a bumping halt, having hit yet another rabbit hole.

With his black singlet, baggy shorts that matched the ancient khaki hat, short woolly socks and stout workboots, Bruce looked every inch the sheep farmer that he was.

He also looked suitably impressed.

'Nice little bird, isn't it?' he greeted Jill. 'Must've cost a pretty penny.'

Jill opened the back door of the Jeep to extract her kit. 'How's the pilot doing?'

'He's alive.' Bruce glanced towards the motionless figure on the hillside. 'And not very polite. Hardly my fault he chose to land in a mob of sheep, is it?'

Jill paused for a moment. Any information Bruce could give her might be helpful in assessing her patient. 'How long was he unconscious?'

'Not long. I was working in the next paddock and saw him come down. Sounded like his engine had conked out. Sheep ran in front of him and he headed for the hill but the wind must've caught it and it flipped. He woke up just after I called for help.' Bruce patted the mobile phone clipped to the pocket of his shorts. 'Never did think much of these newfangled things but I guess they have their uses.'

'How did he get out of the plane?' Jill had started walking towards the man. 'By himself?'

'Yep.' Bruce was staying where he was. 'Sure didn't want my help. Rude blighter if you ask me.'

He's probably got a head injury, Jill thought. Tends to make people seem rude.

'G'day,' she said aloud. 'I'm Jill Metcalf. I'm a doctor.' Taking hold of his wrist, she was pleased to feel a strong, steady pulse.

'Good for you.' He didn't look up.

Jill could see blood oozing between the fingers of the hand cradling his forehead. She unzipped her kit, pulled on a pair of disposable gloves and reached for a dressing and a pouch of saline.

'Are you having any trouble breathing?'

'No.'

'Anything hurting apart from your head?'

'No.'

'What about your neck? Is that sore?'

'No.'

Jill tore open the pouch of fluid and used it to dampen the large gauze pad. 'Let's have a look at the damage.'

'I'm fine.'

'Hey, I'm the doctor here.' Jill kept her tone light. Friendly. 'I'm the one who gets to decide that.'

He resisted for only a moment when she took hold of his hand and lifted it away from his head. She looked at the still bleeding, deep, four-centimetre laceration on his temple.

'You're going to need a few stitches in that.' She put the clean dressing over the wound. 'Hold this on for a tick while I find a bandage.'

The rapid response to her instruction was reassuring. Nothing wrong with his motor skills. With his verbal responsiveness and eye opening good, it put his level of consciousness at normal. She fished in the kit for a crêpe bandage.

'Where the hell am I?'

'Don't you know?' His GCS might need to be amended down a point if he wasn't oriented to time and place. And that could indicate a more serious head injury.

'I didn't notice any signposts, no.'

'Do you remember what happened?' Jill used her teeth to rip open the plastic covering on the bandage.

'I had engine trouble. I was making a perfectly controlled forced landing and a tribe of bloody sheep got in the way, that's what happened. Next thing I knew I was upside down.'

He had a lovely voice. Rich and deep. His clear enunciation suggested a good education.

'You were knocked out,' Jill told him. 'Bruce found you. OK, you can take your hand away now. I've got it.' She held the end of the bandage in place over the dressing and made a loop to secure it. 'Do you know what day it is?'

'Yes.'

Jill continued bandaging in silence for a moment. 'You going to tell me, then?'

'Why? Don't *you* know?'

It should have been irritating, having an uncooperative patient, but there was a hint of humour in the dry tone and it was at that point that the man tilted his head and looked up and Jill could finally see his face properly.

A very striking face. He hadn't shaved for a day or two and there were smears of blood on olive skin that had a hint of pallor but nothing could detract from a pair of absolutely gorgeous, deep brown eyes.

Eyes that reminded her, remarkably vividly, of a pair she'd seen not very long ago, hiding behind some rubbish bins.

Not that they looked anything like dog's eyes, of course. It wasn't even the colour. It was the hint of a haunted look that did it. As though this man, sitting on a hill in a remote sheep paddock, was feeling as lost and abandoned as the dog had been. As though…he had been trying to hide from something that scared him?

Crazy. Her imagination had always been way too keen to run away with her. Jill ignored the way her heart had squeezed in response to the idea that this person was in trouble. Instead, she finished her bandaging, using the little metal clips to secure the end, and focussed on that glint of humour she'd detected. She even smiled cheerfully.

'Yes, I do know what day it is. I'm just trying to find out how well your brain is functioning after the knock you've had on your head.'

'It's the 23rd of December. Two days before Christmas. And it's approximately 12.30 p.m.'

'Closer to 1.30 p.m. now but that's OK. I guess you're oriented. You just don't know where you are.'

'Apart from it being somewhere closer to Wanaka than Dunedin? No.'

'So you were heading for Wanaka?' It was a popular tourist spot.

'Yes.'

'On holiday?'

'Not exactly.' He was looking down. Avoiding both eye contact and the sharing of any personal information. Jill wanted to see his face properly again.

'What's your name?'

'Jack.'

'Really? Hey, I've never met a Jack before.'

'And why is that funny?' He was staring at her with a faintly bewildered air.

Jill did her best to wipe the grin off her face. Maybe she'd been wrong about that sense of humour. 'It's just that…well… I'm Jill, remember?'

The penny dropped quickly enough but he clearly didn't find it amusing and the look Jill received made her feel like an idiot. Hardly professional to be distracted by the childish association their names had with a classic nursery rhyme, was it? Any remnants of her smile vanished and Jill cleared her throat in a businesslike manner.

'I'm going to give you a quick check and then I'll take you back to the hospital so I can sew up your head.'

'Just a ride to town would be good. I need to sort out what to do about my plane.'

'We can deal with that later. There'll be someone at the aero club who'll know what to do.' Jill shone a penlight into Jack's eyes, checking pupil size and reaction. 'You got a headache?'

'Yeah.'

'Feel sick?'

'No.'

Jill felt his head and then his neck. Strangely, it felt like an oddly personal thing to be doing and she'd been a doctor for long enough not to feel like that when treating patients. Was it because of the strange environment—being out in a sheep paddock instead of an emergency department?

Or was it the fact that this Jack was not only an extraordinarily good-looking man but that he'd dropped out of the sky and seemed to be hiding something? It wasn't just her over-active imagination. He was hardly forthcoming in sharing information, was he? He was monosyllabic. Withdrawn. Taciturn, even.

'Let me know if anything hurts,' Jill told him.

Apparently nothing did. With no evidence of any other trauma and his vital signs all within a normal range, Jill was happy to let Jack climb to his feet. She had realised he wasn't a small man but it was disconcerting to be looking up this far. He had to be over six feet tall because Jill's head barely reached his shoulder.

'Take it easy,' she warned. 'I might not be able to catch you if you're too wobbly.'

'I'm fine.' Jack followed her towards the Jeep. He paused beside the plane.

'Thanks,' he said to Bruce. 'Sorry to be nuisance. I'll get the plane out of your paddock as soon as possible.'

Bruce tugged on the floppy brim of his hat. 'No problem, mate. I could give Wally a bell, if ya like.'

Jill came to the rescue in the perplexed silence. 'Wally's in charge at the aero club. He's a retired aircraft engineer so he'll probably be able to help with whatever needs sorting on your plane.'

'Oh…' Jack was staring at the crumpled blade of the propeller. 'That'd be great.'

'He can get hold of Jack at the hospital,' Jill told Bruce. 'We'll be keeping him under observation for a while.' She didn't allow any time for a protest from Jack. The vacant way he was staring at the aircraft was a bit of a worry. 'Let's go, then, shall we?'

'I need my bag. It's in the luggage compartment.' Jack took a step towards the plane but stumbled. Jill caught his arm.

He pulled himself upright and shook off the support. 'I'm all right,' he muttered. 'Just a bit dizzy.'

'Come and sit down, then. In the Jeep,' Jill ordered.

'I'll get your stuff,' Bruce offered.

'There's a pack,' Jack said reluctantly. 'And a camera bag. I really need that.'

Jill made a phone call to cancel the back-up ambulance while Bruce hauled things out of the side compartment of the small plane. The camera bag was large and professional-looking.

'Are you a photographer?' Jill asked.

'Yeah.'

'Freelance?'

Jack was doing up his seat belt. He glanced up at the question and Jill could have sworn he was puzzled. Having trouble coming up with a response. If she was inclined to be uncharitable, it would have been easy to decide that this man was not telling the truth. Then again, he'd had enough of a bump on the head to knock him out. He had admitted to a headache. Maybe he was having trouble with his memory as well.

'Are you on assignment?' she prodded helpfully, 'for a magazine or newspaper or something?'

'No. I'm just working for myself.'

'But you hope to sell your pictures?'

'Um…yeah, I guess.'

Jill gave up. The engine roared into life and she waved at Bruce. As the Jeep bumped back across the paddock away from the farmer and his dogs, a shadowy shape appeared from behind the front seats. Bella's head poked through the gap and she lifted her nose to catch the breeze from the open window.

'Good grief! What's *that*?'

'A dog,' Jill said crisply. 'Her name's Bella. For now.'

She was getting another of those odd looks. 'Do you often change your dog's name, then?'

Jill laughed. 'No. She's just a lost and lonely dog that came into my life about an hour ago. She needed a name.'

'Why Bella?'

'Because she's beautiful.'

Jack gave Bella one of those cautious kind of looks. 'Right.'

'It's OK. She won't bite. At least, I don't think she will.' Jill pulled to a stop and opened her door. 'You stay there. I'll get the gate.'

Bella climbed into the driver's seat while she was out of the vehicle, opening the gate, and when Jill went to get back in she slunk sideways, onto Jack's knee.

'Oof,' he said. 'She doesn't smell very beautiful, does she?'

'Get off, Bella,' Jill ordered. But the dog was still sitting in the same place when she got back from shutting the gate behind them. As they picked up speed, she stood up and thrust her head out the window. Disreputable tawny tufts of hair were instantly plastered against her head. Her rear end was plastered against Jack's chest.

'I could shove her in the back with the kit,' Jill offered.

'I'll survive,' Jack said faintly. 'Takes my mind off my headache, anyway.'

Score one for the mystery man, Jill decided. Not many people would be prepared to have a smelly dog standing on their knee.

'You never told me where I am.'

'Ballochburn,' Jill supplied. 'Heart of stone-fruit country. We're famous for peaches, apricots and cherries. Sheep farming out of the valley. And we've got a lovely river. Favourite holiday spot for hundreds of people. Oh…' Jill braked suddenly. 'And rabbits. We've got millions of rabbits.'

Having avoided squashing the creature, Jill picked up speed again. The new silence was a little disconcerting. And unusual. Jill never had any trouble chatting to anyone but she felt inexplicably wary of this stranger.

She cast frequent glances in her passenger's direction, trying to gauge whether his level of consciousness might be dropping or his wound still bleeding. No eye contact was made. Jack was staring, as best he could, over Bella's back and through the front windscreen.

They were getting into the irrigated land that supported the fruit orchards and it was green and leafy and gorgeous.

'Nice,' Jack murmured.

'It is, isn't it? I haven't been home nearly often enough in the last few years. I forget how glorious it is.'

'You grew up here, then?'

'Yes.' Jill rewarded this voluntary attempt at conversation

with a beaming smile. It was a good sign that her patient wasn't feeling too bad. 'Born and bred. My dad's been the doctor here for thirty-five years.'

'So you're following in his footsteps.'

'Being a doctor? I guess.'

'I meant being here. Is it your turn for the next thirty-five years?'

Jill pulled a face. 'Are you kidding? Fate worse than death in my book. I'm a city girl now. Trained and worked in Auckland and I've got a fabulous job lined up in Melbourne to start in the new year. In Emergency,' she added proudly.

Jack made a sound that fell well below being impressed. 'You like drama, then. Blood and guts.'

'Love it,' Jill said firmly. Somehow, it was disappointing that he wasn't impressed. That he sounded almost derogatory about her chosen passion. 'The bloodier and gutsier, the better.'

No. That made her sound like some kind of trauma vulture. Needing the misfortune of others to spin her wheels.

'I was going to be a GP,' she said more soberly. 'I figured that would fit in with raising a family and stuff down the track, but when I did a run in ED, I just fell in love with it.' Mind you, that could well have had something to do with the fact that her dreams of a settled future and family had been crumbling at the time. No. There was more to her passion than escapism. 'The variety of work is amazing,' she added a little defensively, 'and you actually know that you save a life sometimes.'

'And sometimes you don't.' Jack's tone was flat. Curiously lacking in expression. 'How do you deal with that?'

An odd question. Zeroing in on something negative like that. Was this man haunted and miserable-looking because he had a problem with depression?

'As best you can,' Jill said easily. 'You try and focus on the good stuff.'

Another silence fell but Jill was happy enough to let it continue. Jack's speech was fine. Clear and not repetitive, which could have suggested concussion. He may be unimpressed and negative but his brain seemed to be functioning perfectly well and he wasn't looking nauseated despite the twisting road or the smell wafting from Bella's coat.

He could probably cope if the journey was extended by just a few minutes.

'Would you mind if I stopped up the road here for a tick? There's someone I'd really like to check up on.'

Jack shrugged. 'I'm hardly in a position to object, am I?'

'How are you feeling?'

'Fine.'

'Headache?'

'Hasn't got any worse.'

Jill slowed as the exuberant blooms of a tall rosebush hedge came into view. Sure enough, on a cobbled area in front of some ancient stables, she could see her mother's car parked. She would feel a lot happier if she could reassure herself that all was well with her family.

'I won't be long,' she promised.

She parked in the shade of the hedge, near the black wrought-iron gate that closed a narrow passageway beneath an arch of the roses. Aunty Faith's house had certainly been an original settler's cottage but it had been lovingly restored and added to over the decades and was now nestled in grounds that made it as picturesque as a dwelling could be. It had attracted more than one article in house and garden magazines.

The wide-brimmed straw hat, bobbing amongst the tall

delphinium spires at the back of one of the herbaceous borders, was instantly recognisable. And welcome. There couldn't be too much wrong with someone who was out working in their garden.

'Aunty Faith?'

Jill hurried along a brick path skirting a lawn that looked like a bowling green. She would need to get a lot closer to have any chance of being heard, but she didn't want to give Faith Metcalf too much of a fright. Not when she was ninety-three and could fall off her perch any time.

As if!

Jill was grinning as she rounded the metre-high stand of Shasta daisies and dodged the range of a sprinkler. Nothing frightened her great-aunt. The opposite was far more likely. And how on earth did she stay so immaculate? Her cream gardening gloves looked as unsoiled as her crisp white linen trousers. The Christmas lilies she was clipping with her secateurs wouldn't dare spread their yellow pollen. They were being laid with careful precision to nestle in a long shallow cane basket.

'Hello, Aunty.'

'Jillian! What a lovely surprise.' Faith tilted her cheek to accept a kiss. 'Why aren't you busy doing the clinic?'

'Dad's doing it. I had to go out on a call to an accident.'

'Oh, dear! Nobody badly hurt, I hope?'

'Not too badly. I'm just on my way back to the hospital with him. He needs a few stitches.'

'And you've stopped to say hello?' The tone suggested that Jillian was being remiss in her duties. There was a protocol to almost everything in life as far as Faith was concerned, and it needed to be followed.

'I had to pop in just for a minute,' Jill said apologetically. 'To make sure you were all right.'

'Of course I'm all right. Why wouldn't I be?'

'But Mum's here, isn't she?'

Faith picked up her basket with a sigh. The heady scent of the huge fragrant white lilies floated past Jill's nose. A Christmas smell. These blooms were probably destined for one of her aunt's amazing arrangements that would grace the church or maybe the hospital foyer.

'She's in the gazebo,' Faith confirmed. 'Having a bit of time to herself for once. I'm going to make us some lunch in a minute.'

'I'll just say hello, then.' Jill couldn't shake the vague sense of disquiet the apparently innocuous words had envoked. Since when had her mother hid away in order to have time to herself?

'Didn't you say you had a patient waiting to go to hospital?'

'He's fine for the moment. I've parked in the shade and I'll be really quick.'

He'd fallen into a parallel universe.

One filled with sunshine and birdsong and happy people.

Not that Bruce, the sheep farmer, had been particularly happy but that was understandable as he himself hadn't been all that polite, having found himself hanging upside down in the middle of nowhere.

Great start to a new life. The voyage to rediscover himself and find something meaningful to hang the rest of his life on. Ha!

The fates had decided to rub salt into his wounds, Jack decided, opening his eyes now that the fresh wave of pain and nausea had subsided. The smelly dog had moved, thank goodness. It was curled up on the driver's side. On a seat that was probably still warm from happy, golden Dr Jill's bottom.

A woman who looked like a Christmas angel masquerading as a medic, with that halo of shining blonde curls around blue eyes and a smile that lit up her whole face. Way too happy. And too sure of what path she was following in life. Too capable of dealing with what Jack had failed to deal with so spectacularly.

He blinked, peering out the window as movement caught his peripheral vision. He could see the young doctor walking with a much older woman who was carrying a basket of flowers. He kept staring as the women moved out of view.

He'd been dropped into an environment that looked far too perfect to be real to someone who'd lived in large cities his whole life. Right now he was looking through the bars of a wrought-iron gate at a stone cottage surrounded by an astonishingly colourful garden—a scene that could have graced the front of any coffee-table book or calendar.

It was picture perfect.

So maybe he ought to be taking a picture of it.

He *was* a photographer now, wasn't he?

Yeah….right!

On the other side of the cottage was another smooth green lawn. A stream ran beneath willow trees on the far side and tucked under the graceful foliage was a round trellis structure. A figure got up from the cane chair in the shady interior of the open room.

A woman of about the same height as Jill's petite five feet two but with a much more solid build. Cuddly.

Except she didn't look cuddly right now. Her mother's eyes were swollen and red and her face blotchy. Jill was shocked. The

alarm bell that had sounded faintly at the sight of that cluttered
bench at home was sounding again with a far more strident note.

'Mum! You look awful! What on earth's the matter?'

'Everything!' Hope Metcalf burst into tears.

'Not a very tactful thing to ask, Jillian,' Faith pointed out
mildly.

Jill put her arm around her mother. 'Sorry. I just don't
understand. What's going on?'

'I'm sorry,' her mother sobbed. 'I never meant this to
happen when you've only just got home, but I can't do it any
more…I just can't!'

'Can't do what?'

'Live with your father.'

Jill's jaw dropped. Her parents having marital problems?
It was unthinkable. They were two parts of a single unit. The
core of Jill's rock. The kind of relationship she had confidently
expected to find herself, where the chaff of small irritations
could always be blown away to reveal the wheat of what was
real and important. Could it be that Jill's rock had a previously
unseen crack? Her head moved in a small, decisive shake that
deemed the notion of a major upset ridiculous.

Her great-aunt seemed to agree. 'It's a storm in a teacup,'
she said calmly.

'What is?' The guilt of leaving her patient waiting a
little longer had to be squashed. Jill needed to get to the
bottom of this.

'He shouted at me,' Hope said miserably. 'Just because I
couldn't find his car keys.'

Jill almost smiled. This was hardly the stuff of divorce. Her
father had never been able to find his car keys. Or clean socks.
Or cufflinks or stamps or any of a hundred other things. For

someone who had such a focussed and decisive mind when it came to any matters medical, he had to be the archetypical domestically challenged male.

'And he should have told me years ago how much he resented the children. He always said if it made me happy then it made *him* happy.'

'Of course it did,' Faith said soothingly. 'He didn't mean it, Hope. James has always been very proud of the lengths you went to to help all those children.'

Jill had thought so, too. Or had that been an illusion? Like her parents' marriage being rock solid and unshakable?

'No.' Hope pressed a damp handkerchief to her nose. 'He said he's never had a home to call his own. It's always been full of waifs and strays and troublemakers. He said, just for once, he'd like to have the house to himself for Christmas. Well, that's what he's going to get.'

'Oh…' Jill took a deep and somewhat shaky breath. She hadn't thought for a moment that dropping in here would be lifting the lid on a giant can of worms.

Totally unexpected worms that she couldn't begin to try and unravel right now.

'We need to talk about this, Mum, but I can't stay right now. I've got a man in the Jeep who needs stitches in his head. What time will you be home?'

'I'm not coming home.'

Faith patted Jill's arm. 'You go, my dear. Look after your patient. I'll look after your mother.'

'But…'

The pat became pressure. Jill found herself moving along the path towards the front gate, accompanied by both her great-aunt and her mother.

Her mobile phone rang. She looked at the call display a little helplessly. Did her father have any idea of how much he'd upset his wife?

'Hi, Dad,' she answered warily.

'Where the hell are you?'

'I'm on my way back. I just stopped to make sure Aunty Faith was all right as I was going past.'

'Do you have any idea where your mother is?'

'Yes.' This was good. Maybe he wanted to apologise for whatever outburst had triggered this unprecedented disharmony. 'She's right here. Do you want to talk to her?'

Her mother was glaring as she shook her head firmly. Her father sounded even more determined.

'No, I don't,' he said furiously. 'Just tell her that she'd better get home. That blasted woman from Invercargill just turned up with four children she wants to leave here. *Four!*' The call was cut off abruptly.

Judging by the shocked look on Hope's face, she had heard the angry words quite clearly.

'It must be Margaret,' she said in dismay, 'but I told her this morning I would have to think about it. That I'd ring her back after I'd talked to Jim. That's what started all the trouble and then I was so upset I forgot all about it.'

'It's not the best time to have a whole family that needs fostering, is it?' Jill chewed her lip anxiously. 'I'll talk to Margaret when I get back.'

Faith didn't appear to be listening. She was frowning as she neared the gate. 'Who is that?'

Jill's eyebrows rose. 'That's my patient. From the plane crash.'

'What's he doing?'

'Looks like he's taking photographs.'

'Well, obviously, Jillian. I may be old but I'm not senile. I'd just like to know why he's taking photographs of my house without asking my permission.'

'He's got a head injury.' Jill felt obliged to defend Jack. 'He probably forgot.'

Introductions seemed to be in order, although it felt very strange when this man was a patient.

'This is my mother, Hope Metcalf,' Jill said cautiously, 'and my great-aunt, Faith.' She turned to her family. 'This is Jack…'

The pause was unavoidable. An introduction to someone without a surname would not be up to scratch. Sure enough, Faith stared down her nose.

'Jack who?'

'Sinclair,' he provided, willingly enough. 'Pleased to meet you, ma'am.'

Nice manners, Jill thought approvingly. Might help if he smiled sometimes, though. She noted the faint bloodstain on the bandage around Jack's head. It was high time she got him back to the hospital and fixed that wound properly. She'd better remember to ask when he'd last had a tetanus shot as well.

'You're taking photographs of my house,' Faith was saying sternly. 'Why?'

'It's an extraordinarily beautiful house,' Jack responded. 'I've never seen anything like it.'

Faith was only partially mollified. 'What do you intend doing with those photographs?'

'Nothing.' Jack put his camera back into the bag. 'But I'm sure I'll enjoy seeing it again. I could send you some copies if you like.'

'Hmm.' The sound was suspicious. 'What do you normally take photographs of, Mr Sinclair?'

Jill expected a vague answer like the one she'd received when trying to quiz Jack about his profession, but to her surprise Jack's lips quirked into something hinting at a smile as he met her great-aunt's steely gaze.

'I was planning to do a series about Christmas,' he said. 'To see if I could capture something unique. Traditionally Kiwi, you know? I'd like to try and record what makes it special.'

'He was heading for Wanaka, Aunty,' Jill put in. 'But his plane crashed.'

'It didn't *crash*,' Jack corrected her. 'I was making a perfectly well-controlled forced landing…'

'And then you crashed.' Jill wasn't going to let him avoid the truth. She'd have to watch that he didn't make light of any symptoms that could point to a head injury that needed investigation.

'Hmm,' Faith said again. It was a thoughtful sound now. 'You do look a bit pale, Mr Sinclair. I think you'd better get to the hospital and let Jillian sort you out.'

Her mother, who had been struggling valiantly to look happy and interested in meeting Jack, couldn't control the wobble of her bottom lip. 'And the children, Jilly. Please, tell Margaret I'm dreadfully sorry but…'

Faith linked her arm through Hope's and turned her away from the gate. 'Jillian's more than capable of sorting everything out. It's high time we had a cup of tea, my dear.'

Bella reluctantly made room as they got back into the Jeep.

'It's not far now.' Jill tried to sound cheerful which wasn't easy, given the new crisis brewing that she was supposed to sort out on top of the shocking revelation that her parents were a lot less than happy with each other. She started the engine and pulled back onto the road. 'Less than ten minutes. I must apologise for that.'

'Why?'

'Hardly very professional to go visiting when I'm effectively driving an ambulance. I've…ah…got a small family crisis going on.'

Jack grunted. 'Your mother certainly didn't look very happy.'

'No.' For a wild moment Jill was tempted to tell this stranger everything. To spill out how disturbing it was to have a crack appearing in her rock. But that would be even less professional than going visiting during a patient transport, wouldn't it? Besides, Jack looked as though he had problems of his own. He couldn't possibly be interested in having someone else's dumped on him.

But it was Jack who broke the silence that fell. 'So why isn't she happy?'

Maybe he *was* interested. Maybe if she was open with him, he might reciprocate. You shouldn't expect to receive more than you were prepared to give, should you?

'Things are a bit stressed,' she said carefully. 'The practice here covers a fairly vast area and there's a population of around three thousand people, which goes up considerably over the summer holiday period. It needs at least two doctors to manage but the last locum left six months ago and Dad's been coping on his own. He's sixty-five now so he should be thinking about retiring, but he can't. Not unless he can find a replacement and that's not going to be easy. Bad enough having a huge general practice with no after-hours relief, but there's the hospital to run on top of that.'

'What size is the hospital?'

'Not big at all. It used to have a thirty-bed capacity and facilities for minor surgery and stuff, but it's been downgraded. There's always a few elderly, recuperative and maternity patients, though, and the locals are determined not to lose the service. Anyway, I think Dad's tired and overworked and he's managed to upset Mum, which is a bit of a worry. Not what I expected when I came home for a happy family Christmas.'

'I guess not. And now you need to smooth things out for your siblings?'

'I don't have any siblings.'

'Your mother said something about the children. About telling Margaret how sorry she is.'

'Oh… Margaret's a social worker. From Invercargill. The children will be cases who need fostering. Mum's been taking in foster-children for ever.'

'*You* were a foster-child?' Jack sounded stunned.

'No, but I was supposed to be the first of about six, and that didn't happen. When I was about eight or nine Mum got interested in fostering and we've had extras in the house at times ever since.'

Waifs and strays and troublemakers.

A crying baby sometimes. A toddler marching around on fat little legs at other times. Quiet children and surly teenagers. They had stayed anywhere from a few days to a few months usually, though Maria had been there until the age of sixteen—even after they'd discovered she had been stealing drugs from the surgery and trying to sell them on the internet.

'They weren't all troublemakers,' she said aloud. 'And it was hardly continuous. Ballochburn's well off the beaten track so my parents weren't at the top of any list of available foster-parents. I suspect what's happened is that there's been a request for a placement over Christmas and, on top of the workload, it's a bit much for Dad right now. The children will just have to go somewhere else, I guess.'

Jack grunted again. He didn't sound interested any more and Jill drove in silence, giving up the hope that he might want to start talking about himself. It was curiously disappointing. Almost embarrassing. She was too open sometimes, wasn't she? Too trusting of people. She should have learned her lessons by now and yet she still got overruled by her instincts about people. The need to get involved.

Jack Sinclair clearly didn't want to let her into any part of his life. She may be rescuing him and on the way to patch up his wounds, but that would be it. He would exit her life, leaving an air of mystery behind him.

But again it was Jack who broke the silence. With another question that was a little out of left field.

'So your real name is Jillian, huh?'

'I hate it,' Jill said, with feeling. 'But I really can't complain.'

'Why not?'

'Because I narrowly escaped being called Glory.'

He had to think about that for a second and then he huffed. The sort of sound someone might make if they had no intention of being amused but couldn't help it.

'Right…an aunt Faith and a mother Hope. Yeah…you *were* lucky.'

This time the quirk of his lips was nearly half a smile. Jill turned her head at just the right moment to catch it and she was startled. If this man *really* smiled, he would be… gorgeous.

Absolutely, stunningly gorgeous.

An odd sensation pierced her gut. A weird *ping* that, unfortunately, Jill recognised only too easily.

Uh-oh!

There was something seriously attractive about Jack Sinclair.

Danger signs flashed with neon brightness in her head. It was as much a part of who she was as her overactive imagination and her willingness to trust others. Not that she felt that attracted to many men—quite the opposite, given that it had only happened a very few times—but when it did, it was like a runaway horse. She could fall in love so hard it blinded her, and by the time she found she'd been attracted to the wrong person, it was way too late.

It was *not* going to happen again.

No way.

Jill's fierce grip on the steering-wheel only eased as she pulled into the hospital car park.

'Here we are,' she said with forced brightness.

At least distraction was at hand. Beside a station wagon marked with the insignia of the southern health region's social welfare department, an anxious-looking woman stood talking to Jill's father.

Behind the woman were four children.

And three of them were crying.

CHAPTER THREE

THE misery of the children must be contagious.

Jim Metcalf had obviously caught it. He glared at his daughter.

'Where's your mother?'

'She can't come.'

'Why not?'

Jill's look told her father that she was far enough in the loop to know that he knew the answer to that question perfectly well. He looked disconcerted but then frowned. Jill groaned inwardly. Whatever the argument had been about, her father had decided he was in the right and she knew just how stubborn he was capable of being about backing down. Her mother could also be stubborn. No wonder she hadn't been able to escape that particular family trait.

'If I could just talk to her,' the anxious-looking woman said. 'I know I shouldn't have just come but I thought if she *met* the children…'

Jill looked at the wall of children. The only one not crying was the oldest—a sulky-looking boy of about nine or ten. Dark-skinned, with black hair, he was nothing like the smaller boy, who had red hair, or the girl, who had blonde hair but blazingly red cheeks. She was clutching the hand of a toddler who had virtually no hair at all and who was shrieking loudly enough to have brought Maisie out from the kitchens.

'What on earth is all this racket about?' Maisie demanded.

Jill was aware that Jack had climbed out of the Jeep. This was embarrassing. Not only was her passenger not particularly interested in any stress her family was under, he'd been less than impressed with the direction she was taking her medical career and he was now going to stand and watch her try to sort out what could only be described as a small circus happening in the car park of this sleepy rural hospital.

'It's OK, Maisie. I'll sort it out.' Jill tried to sound confident.

Maisie snorted.

Bella had climbed out of the vehicle to follow Jack. The toddler's shrieks made her cringe but she slunk closer to Jill and sat down on her foot. For a skinny dog, she was surprisingly heavy.

So was the heat of this summer's day. Jill could feel it pressing on her head like another weight. Heavy enough to cause discomfort that threatened to turn into a nasty headache. No wonder the children all looked hot and miserable. It would have been a drive of several hours to bring them here from Invercargill.

Something had to be done.

'Could you take the children into the kitchen and give them all a cold drink, please, Maisie?'

The cook blinked at Jill's firm tone but then gave a small nod, as though pleasantly surprised. She began to herd the children but couldn't resist a look over her shoulder.

'Have you fed that poor dog yet?'

'No.' Jill looked down at her foot. 'Bella, go with Maisie. She'll find you some food.'

Another snort was heard from Maisie's direction but the oldest boy paused and turned to stare at Bella. Bella stared back.

'Go on,' Jill urged. 'There's a good girl.'

The boy tapped his hand on his leg. Bella gave Jill a questioning look and Jill nudged her with her foot. 'Go on,' she encouraged.

Bella disappeared in the wake of the procession heading for the kitchens. Jim cleared his throat and looked longingly at the direction he needed to take to get back inside the main hospital building.

'I really ought to get back to my patients,' he grumbled. 'I've got Judith Cartwright in there with chest pain.'

Jill gave her father another look. Judith Cartwright was probably hyperventilating from stress. Again. It was hardly life-threatening. 'Could you show Jack where the waiting room is?' Jill gestured towards the man standing silently to one side. 'He was KO'd and could be concussed. He's also got a laceration that needs suturing.'

'It'll be a while before I have time to deal with that.' Jim ran his fingers through his thick salt-and-pepper hair, ruffling it enough to rival Bella's tufts. 'I've got a packed waiting room as it is.'

'I'm fine,' Jack said. 'There's absolutely no rush.'

'I'll do the suturing,' Jill promised. 'And I'll be able to help with the rest of clinic. Just give me ten minutes to sort things out.'

'Good.' Jim nodded and gave Jack a curious glance. 'I'll leave you for Jill to look after, then.' He smiled, nodded at Margaret then turned with obvious relief to march purposefully off towards the main doors.

'I'm so sorry,' Margaret said. 'I really didn't mean to cause such a problem. It's just that Hope's always been so helpful and I was desperate. There's no way I can keep this family together if we have to place them in town.'

Jill eyebrows rose. 'They're from one family?'

'Yes. They've all got different fathers.' The social worker sighed. 'I've known the mother for quite a while. She died this morning quite unexpectedly.'

'Oh, that's awful! What happened to her?'

'She overdosed on her antidepressants. We're trying to trace her family but they've gone on holiday somewhere in Europe so it's proving difficult. It could be a week or more until we can make proper arrangements and it seemed a bit tough to separate the children at Christmas.'

Of course it was. Jill chewed her lip. She could offer to take them home herself but that was hardly going to help sort things out for her parents, was it?

'I wish I could help,' she said slowly, 'but the problem is that Mum's not at home at the moment.'

'When will she be back?'

'I really don't know,' Jill answered honestly. 'I'm not sure she knows herself.' She avoided looking at Jack to see how he was reacting to her evasion. He knew her mother wasn't far away. Would he think her completely heartless, sending these children back to the city to get separated and sent to different foster-homes? He was already unimpressed with her. Seeing disappointment would be even worse.

Margaret sighed. 'It's not your fault, dear. I knew it was a gamble. I'll just have to take them back to town. Poor things, they hated the drive up. In fact, they haven't stopped crying since the police collected them all this morning.'

'I'm not surprised. They've just lost their mother.'

'The little ones don't really know what's going on but I'm worried about Jarred—the oldest. He's only nine and he's been holding that family together for a long time. He'll be devastated if they get split up.'

'I hope you can find the family soon.'

'So do I.' Margaret didn't sound very hopeful and Jill had to fight the urge to try and make everything all right. To say that, of course, her mother would love to help. But that was impossible. There was no way she could make this all right for everybody concerned.

Instead, she cleared her throat. 'I'll show you where the kitchens are,' she said. 'Jack? You may as well come with us and get out of this sun. I'll take you through to the surgery when we've found the children.'

Maisie was standing in the middle of the kitchen, her arms folded. 'If you ask me, these children are sick,' she said indignantly. 'You could fry an egg on the head of that baby.'

'Really?' Jill moved swiftly to lay her hand on the wispy hair. 'You're right, Maisie.'

She turned to the girl whose tear-stained cheeks were still flushed scarlet, despite being out of the sun. 'Hello, sweetheart. What's your name?'

'J-Jade.'

'Are you feeling sick, Jade?'

'I want Mummy,' the girl sobbed.

The oldest boy, Jarred, was crouched beside Bella, who was licking the base of a stainless-steel basin. He looked up.

'We've all been sick,' he said sullenly. 'We've got spots.'

'Oh, Lord!' Margaret sank onto a chair beside the long table. 'I had no idea.'

Jack stayed near the door he had just entered. He put his bags down and was watching the scene with apparent interest.

'What sort of spots?' Jill asked. 'Can you show me?'

'I can.' The red-haired boy hoisted up his T-shirt. 'I've got the most.'

Jill stared at the skinny pale chest on view. A chest that was marked by the outline of ribs but also by a lot of angry red dots. She moved closer. Some of the dots had little blisters on them.

'Oh…' Jill took a deep, even breath. 'And you've all got these spots?'

'Nat hasn't got any,' Jarred said, pointing at the toddler. 'And mine are starting to go kind of scabby now.'

'I've got more than Jarred had,' the redhead proclaimed. 'And they're really, really itchy.'

'Chickenpox,' Maisie announced triumphantly. 'I'd know those kind of spots anywhere.'

'What's your name?' Jill asked. Why hadn't she noticed the spots among his freckles earlier?

'Mel.'

'After Mel Gibson,' Jarred said. A rather adult tone of disparagement was clear. 'Mum thought he was hot.'

Jade's sobs increased in intensity. 'I want *Mummy*.'

Margaret looked ready to cry herself. 'Is that what it is? Chickenpox?'

'Yes.' Jill was nodding thoughtfully. 'It's chickenpox all right.'

'This is terrible,' Margaret said faintly. 'We can't place the children in private homes if they're contagious.' She paused and gulped audibly. '*Are* they contagious?'

'Very,' Jill said. 'The infectious period is from one to two days before the appearance of the rash until it's fully crusted.'

She smiled at the children. 'But don't worry. You'll all feel better in a few days.'

'But….' Margaret was clearly at a loss. 'What am I going to do?'

Jill smiled again. What needed to be done was crystal clear as far as she was concerned.

Maisie looked at Jill and sighed deeply.

Jack was also watching her. It seemed likely that he'd guessed her thoughts, judging by the suggestion of an incredulous smile that was tugging at his mouth.

He *wanted* to smile properly, didn't he? It was almost as though he'd forgotten how to.

'These children are sick,' Jill said calmly. 'They need to stay together and they have nowhere to go. I'm going to admit them all to hospital.'

'In Invercargill?' Margaret queried. Her eyes widened at the prospect of another long journey with a carload of children she now knew to be unwell.

'No,' Jill said. 'Here. In Ballochburn.'

Maisie made an 'I knew it' grumbling sound.

'We've got plenty of empty beds,' Jill said firmly. 'And we can call in some extra staff to help.'

Maisie's grumble took on a 'you'll be lucky' tone now.

'They can all stay together,' Jill continued, unable to prevent sounding pleased with herself. 'We'll open up one of the four-bed wards next to Maternity. I'll just call one of our nurses and get the beds made up.'

'How long will they need to stay in hospital?'

'Until they're not contagious. Could be anywhere from five to ten days. At least a week, anyway.'

Long enough for Margaret to have a chance to sort a

suitable and more permanent arrangement. Long enough to keep the children together, at least for Christmas. The social worker caught Jill's eye and smiled.

'Thank you,' she said softly. 'You're an angel.'

'Why did you do that?'

Jack was walking beside Jill along a quiet central corridor. The hospital had been built in an era that had taken aesthetics into account as much as any practical considerations. The high plaster ceilings were decorated with ornate roses along the edges. The floor was of deep brown polished wood and the long, wide space was punctuated at regular intervals with moulded wooden archways. Tall sash windows afforded a view into a well-tended garden.

'You didn't have to,' Jack added. He sounded curious rather than disapproving. Puzzled, even.

'It was the perfect solution.' Jill gave a satisfied sigh. 'Dad can hardly object—not when they're sick. He's good with sick people—especially children.'

'One would hope so,' Jack murmured.

'And Mum will be delighted. She'd feel terrible letting Margaret down and she'd move heaven and earth to help children in that sort of predicament. This way, she can help look after them but they won't be at home so it can't make things any worse there.'

'Things are bad at home?'

'Ah…' Jill had allowed her pleasure at solving one crisis to loosen her tongue more than she'd intended. 'Not really. Like I told you, there's a bit of stress around at the moment, that's all. It's nothing major.'

At least, she hoped it was nothing major. She slowed, glad

of a reason not to think about her mother's tear-ravaged face.
'Come in here. We've got a good treatment room next to
X-Ray. It should have everything we need to fix up your
head.' She grinned up at Jack. 'I'll spare you the trauma of
going through the waiting room and being the subject of avid
interest to all our locals.'

'Small town, huh?'

'Yes. Although we get quite a few strangers at this time of
year. The camping ground is a real favourite and it's amazing
how many people can get sick or injured on holiday. Not
really fair, is it? A hospital is the last place you'd want to be
when you're on your summer holidays.'

A hospital was the last place Jack wanted to be, full stop.

The corridor had been OK. So unlike the kind of hospital
environment Jack was used to that it hardly registered.

But here, in this treatment room, it felt like the walls were
closing in. Everything was so familiar. Too familiar. The
oxygen and entonox cylinders, the trays of IV gear, the boxes
of disposable gloves. Even the smell.

Jack climbed onto the bed that Jill was patting. He lay back
and closed his eyes with a faint groan.

'You're not feeling great, are you?'

What an understatement!

'Not particularly,' Jack said through gritted teeth.

'Head hurting?'

'It's OK.'

'Feeling sick?'

'No.'

'What's making you feel so bad, then?'

She sounded like she cared. Really cared. But Jack didn't

want her sympathy. Didn't need it. He almost laughed. Life, he felt like saying. The fact that I'm so burnt out I'm dead inside. I have nothing left to give so why should I expect to be given anything myself?

Christmas. The season of giving.

And Jack had landed in the middle of nowhere to find a Christmas angel who seemed to be spreading magic.

That smelly dog thought so, anyway.

And four hot, miserable, itchy children.

And that worried-looking social worker from down south.

It was crazy and Jack was miserable enough to find the good humour and altruism irritating. So was the confidently expectant silence from Jill.

'I just don't like Christmas,' he growled finally.

'Ooh!' He could hear the smile. 'A real live Grinch. Cool!'

She obviously wasn't taking him seriously. He could hear a kind of hum as she moved around, collecting what she needed. A Christmas carol he vaguely recognised. Was it intended as a reproach to his 'Bah, humbug' comment? Jack focussed on the other sounds. Packages being ripped open. The clink of things dropping onto a tray or kidney dish. The sound of water running as Jill scrubbed her hands. Then he could sense her coming closer. Could feel her warmth and smell the faint scent of something like strawberries. Could feel the gentle touch of her hands as she began unwinding the bandage from around his head.

'Do you have any medical conditions I should know about, Jack?'

'No.' Except maybe post-traumatic stress syndrome. Or possibly good, old-fashioned, everyday depression.

'Are you taking any medication on a regular basis?'

'No.' They'd been offered, of course. Advocated strongly,

in fact, but Jack had been horrified. He'd take time out first, he'd said. Six months or a year. See if he could sort out his head himself. And his heart.

'When did you last have a tetanus booster?'

'About ten years ago.' He'd had one when he'd started working in an emergency department, hadn't he? Along with the course of hepatitis vaccine. You could take precautions against some of the potential dangers of working on the front line, couldn't you?

Shame there wasn't a vaccine to prevent getting too involved emotionally.

Getting wrecked.

Dying inside.

He could have carried on. Like the consultant he'd worked under, Jack could have functioned so that medicine had just been a job. No involvement. No caring. No fallout when things went wrong because that was just part of the job. You won some, you lost some.

But that had been, quite simply, unacceptable.

If he was incapable of becoming involved—in a controlled fashion so that he, at least, cared about what he was doing— then he would get out completely.

For ever.

Right now it felt like he could never be involved on any level. There was nothing left to give.

Just an empty space.

Sucking in a sharp breath was involuntary but Jack actually welcomed the sting of the fluid in his wound. It made him feel alive.

'Sorry,' Jill said. 'I'll put a bit of local in now. You'll feel it stinging a bit.'

It did sting.

And then there was just numbness.

The kind of numbness he was almost getting used to on an emotional level.

Jack cracked his eyes open far enough to catch a glimpse of Jill as she worked.

She was gorgeous—even with no hint of that merry smile creasing her face. Concentration on her task had intensified the blue of her eyes so that they reminded him of the tall delphinium spires he had seen in her great-aunt's garden. He could see the freckles dusting pale skin and decorating a cute snubbed nose. And the enchanting way her bottom lip was caught, just at one side, between small white teeth.

At any other time in his life Jack would have found this woman astonishingly attractive.

Right now he would have welcomed an indication of a response that was more than purely intellectual in the same way he'd appreciated the sting of the local anaesthetic. But it was like looking at a photograph. An attractive picture of something he had absolutely no connection with.

Being this close let him notice that pale band of skin on the third finger of her left hand where it was obvious a ring had been worn for a long time but had now been removed, suggesting that Jill was single again. Even that couldn't prompt any more than a vague surprise that she'd had a relationship that hadn't worked out.

Fear threatened to step in again.

The fear that he might have lost the ability to connect with anybody.

And what made that so terrifying was the knowledge that

the ability to connect was the only thing that could give life any real meaning.

Jack had to close his eyes again. To try and focus on the painless tugging he could feel happening to the skin on the side of his forehead. It was easy to imagine himself standing behind young Dr Metcalf, watching what she was doing.

Putting the needle in far enough from the edge of the wound to prevent the suture from tearing through the skin.

Releasing the needle holder and grasping the tip of the needle with forceps to pull it out of the base of the wound. Inserting it into the base of the opposite side and pushing it to the surface.

Pulling the suture material through and looping it twice around the needle holder. Grasping the short end and pulling it through the loops.

He could feel the wound edges being drawn together as the first knot was tied.

Stay focussed, he warned himself.

Don't step back any further.

Because, if he did, he would see the bigger picture of the young, vibrantly alive woman caring for an empty shell of a man.

And Jack didn't want to see that man. It wasn't him.

If he didn't sink into the fear, he could hold onto the hope that he could find what he'd lost.

He could find himself again.

CHAPTER FOUR

'WHAT have you done with that plane-crash fellow?'

'I got Maisie onto him.' Blonde curls bounced as Jill shook her head ruefully on entering the consulting room. 'I had to take extreme measures. He wasn't about to take my advice and rest quietly for a few hours.' She grinned. 'I finally told him I didn't have time to do the paperwork until I'd helped you with the clinic and if he scarpered I'd get into big trouble. The hospital might get its licence revoked and I was sure he didn't want to be responsible for having Ballochburn's iconic medical facility closed down. Besides, he needed a cup of tea and something for his headache.'

'Could do with a cup of tea myself, 'Jim grumbled. 'I popped into the kitchen a while back but Maisie was nowhere to be seen.'

'Mmm.' Jill tried to sound both surprised and sympathetic but she knew perfectly well that Maisie would have been upstairs, helping to make up beds for the new inpatients her father clearly didn't know about yet. Time to change the subject. 'Who would you like me to see?'

Her father finished the sentence he was scribbling in a patient's file. Jill could see the pink paper of an ECG trace so he must have taken Judith's chest pain seriously enough to investigate it properly.

'Check with Muriel that nothing urgent has come in. If not, young Aaron Baker's got a sore arm. Doesn't look broken so he wasn't top of the list but he's been waiting awhile. If you sort him, I'll get on with all the repeat prescriptions. Sue's coming in as well. She's running a bit low on morphine.'

'Oh, I must catch up with Sue. I feel terrible I haven't had a chance to get out to the orchard yet.'

'I'll tell her you're here. She needs her friends right now and no mistake. She's having one tough year.'

'I know. We saw a lot of each other when she was up in Auckland with Emma.'

A tiny silence fell. A look shared that made Jill swallow hard to get rid of the sudden lump in her throat. What could you say when your best friend was facing the final Christmas her small child would ever have?

She managed a smile. Hopefully one that let her father know she understood how tough his part in the story was. That she was aware of the stress levels and that the grumpiness that might have upset the apple cart at home was forgivable. That she loved him for the depth of involvement and the genuine care he gave his patients. A quality she'd thought she'd found in the man she'd married, only she'd been very wrong. He had cared far more for himself than anyone else.

Many of those patients were still crowding the small waiting area. Jill had a quick word with Muriel, the receptionist, and then took Aaron and his mother and a melted bag of frozen peas through to the treatment room. Jim took Mrs Briggs into the consulting room. There were still half a dozen people sitting patiently, thumbing through magazines that were probably years out of date. Except for the large girl in the corner, who was sitting motionless, her head down and her long hair screening her face. But Jill couldn't respond to the subtle warning bell ringing in the back of her head. Not when there was obviously nothing life-threatening going on.

'Your dad was a friend of mine,' she told six-year-old Aaron. 'I went to school with him and I seem to remember him hurting *his* arm once. He fell off his motorbike. You're not into motorbikes yet, are you?'

Aaron's mother groaned. 'He would be if he got half a chance but, no, this time it was Rambo's fault.'

'Rambo?' Jill lifted the small boy to sit on the edge of the bed that Jack had been occupying only minutes previously. The tray of things she'd used to suture that laceration was still sitting on the bench, waiting to be cleaned up.

She could still feel his presence.

That odd sensation of too personal a contact that had come from touching him.

The curiosity about why he didn't like Christmas.

'Rambo's my lamb,' Aaron said proudly. 'We were practising.'

'It's pets' day tomorrow,' his mother said. 'Rambo's supposed to walk nicely for the judging and in the parade only he's grown like a weed and he's a bit strong for Aaron now. He pulled him over.'

'Where does it hurt?' Jill asked.

'Here.' Aaron pointed at his forearm.

'Can you wiggle your fingers?'

Small and very grubby fingers waggled.

'Can you squeeze my hand?'

'Ouch!'

'Show me where that hurts.'

Jill made a thorough examination of the limb. 'I don't think anything's broken,' she concluded. 'It's a bit sore but it isn't too swollen and it's not restricting his movement too much. If it gets worse we'll need to take an X-ray but I'm confident it's just a sprain. A bandage and some rest should do the trick. The bag of peas was a brilliant idea—it would have helped a lot.'

'Can I still take Rambo to pets' day?'

'Can Mum or Dad help you when it comes to the parade?'

'I don't *want* help. I'm not a baby.'

Jill nodded. 'Of course you're not. You'd have to be careful not to let him hurt your arm any more, though. Maybe you could just let him go if he pulls too hard, instead of trying to hang onto him.' She smiled at Aaron's mother. 'I guess the worst thing that could happen is that Rambo will run amok and cause chaos.'

'Which half the pets will be doing anyway!'

'Yeah.' Jill's smile broadened as she opened a crêpe bandage and began winding it around the small wrist.

She had to push aside the memory of winding another crêpe bandage so recently…around Jack's head. She had to stop letting him enter her mind so often or it could get out of control. Given her track record, her imagination could run amok far more wildly than Rambo ever could. She'd be having visions of walking down an aisle on Jack's arm soon. Admiring the wall of professional photographs he'd taken of their six beautiful children. Having the anticipation of seeing him smile to help get her through the worst of any working days.

Oh, *help*! Just the thought of seeing that smile was enough to make her feel gooey inside. This was threatening to be a bad dose.

'I took a pet lamb to school one year,' she said, a trifle desperately. 'Someone's dog started chasing it and they went right into the classrooms.'

Aaron's eyes widened. He was impressed. 'Did you get into trouble?'

'Not really. I had to clean up the little present he'd left for the teacher, though.'

Aaron giggled. 'What was *your* lamb's name?'

'Minty.' Jill wasn't going to elaborate. It had been her father's idea to call the orphan Mint Sauce. Lamb Chops had been the previous year's model.

'Are you coming tomorrow?'

'I'll certainly try. What time is the parade?'

'Two p.m.,' Aaron's mother supplied. 'And then there's the barbecue and school break-up.'

'That would bring back a few memories.' Jill sighed happily. ' I hope I can make it.'

'Will you bring a pet?' Aaron asked.

'I haven't got one at the moment. Although…' Jill taped the end of the bandage into place. 'I did find a dog today. If I brought her to school, someone might recognise her and I could find her owner.' She lifted Aaron back to the floor. 'Mind you, she'd need a bath first. She's a bit stinky.'

'So's Rambo.' Aaron looked up at his mother. 'Can we give *him* a bath?'

'No.'

'Please?'

'He's a sheep, Aaron. Sheep don't get in the bath.'

'But he's my *pet*!' Aaron's lip wobbled. 'And I want him to *win* and I can't wash him by myself because I've got a sore *arm*…'

Aaron's mother sighed deeply. 'We'll see…'

Mrs Briggs was coming out of the consulting room, clutching a prescription, as Jill waved the Bakers off.

'My Wally's coming in later,' she was saying to her doctor. 'There's a Friends of the Hospital meeting this evening.'

'Is there?' Jill's father didn't sound thrilled. Yet another evening to be taken up with professional responsibilities.

'Yes. Six-thirty p.m. You will be there, won't you, Dr Metcalf?'

'Probably,' Jim said gloomily.

'I'll be there,' Jill said. 'Did Wally get the message about that plane, Mrs Briggs?'

'Yes. He went to have a look at it after he dropped me off here.'

'I'll bring Jack to the meeting, then. He can have a chat to Wally.'

'And Hope will be there, of course?'

'Don't ask me,' Jim snapped.

'I'm sure she will.' Jill shot her father a warning glance as Mrs Briggs's eyebrows shot up. 'She wouldn't miss the Christmas meeting. Not when you always bring those wonderful mince pies of yours.'

Mrs Briggs sniffed. 'Yes, well, Wally'd better hurry up so I can get home to bake them. I'll look forward to seeing Hope later, then.'

'Mmm.' At least her mother wouldn't be too far away from the meeting venue. The quick phone call Jill had managed earlier had set wheels in motion so easily it only confirmed that she'd done the right thing. Hope would be upstairs somewhere right now, getting those children settled and happy. Finding pyjamas and toys and books. Probably a television set and videos. Planning on how to help Maisie feed them all.

Very satisfying.

Apart from the unexploded bomb of her father not being consulted about admitting four cases of chickenpox to his hospital.

Jill avoided his eye. 'Who's next, then?'

'Can you take that girl in the corner? I have no idea who she is.'

Doreen Briggs peered over her spectacles. 'Not a local,' she pronounced. 'Must be a camper.'

The girl's name was Elise. She followed Jill though to the treatment room without taking her eyes off the floor in front of her feet.

'Are you here on holiday, Elise?'

'Nah. I just got a ride with some people who were going camping here.'

'Where have you come from?'

'Dunedin.'

'Does your family know you're here?'

'Nah.'

The tone made it clear that the line of questioning wasn't welcome. Jill backed off.

'How old are you, Elise?'

'Eighteen.'

The eye contact was fleeting but defensive. She didn't look eighteen. Had she picked that as an age in order to stop someone trying to contact her family?

'And what's brought you in here today? Are you not feeling well?'

'I'm fine.'

Yet again, Jack popped into Jill's head. He'd kept saying he was fine when it had been painfully obvious he hadn't been. This girl was giving off a similar kind of vibe, too. Something sad. Something they were hiding…running away from.

'So how can I help?' she asked gently.

'I had a job in Dunedin,' Elise said. 'I was a nurse aide in an old folks' home. I've got a reference.'

'That's good.' Jill smiled, encouraging the girl to keep talking. To tell her what problem had brought her to seek medical assistance.

Elise looked up. She hesitated but then smiled back and for a moment the misery in her face vanished. If she washed her hair, Jill thought, and got a bit of sunshine and a healthy diet, and some clothes that weren't baggy enough to look like sacks, she would be a stunning-looking young woman.

'So, will you give me a job, then?'

'Ah…' Jill hadn't expected that. 'Is *that* why you're here?'

'Yeah. I really need a job.'

Jill nodded slowly. Lots of young people flocked to Central Otago for summer employment. There were always vacancies at the orchards.

'But why here?' she said aloud. 'In a hospital? Why not outside in one of the orchards? Or in a packing shed where there'd be heaps of kids your age?'

'I like hospitals,' Elise said. 'I want to be a nurse one day. You wanna see my reference?'

'OK.' Jill was trying to buy thinking time. She'd already

landed her father with a virtually one hundred per cent increase in the number of inpatients. If she started hiring casual staff behind his back, he would have just cause to regret asking her to help out as his locum. Not to mention that he was feeling aggrieved at the way waifs and strays had peppered his life. Elise had to fall into the stray camp. She was a bit solid to be a waif.

But Maisie had been looking for part-time help in the kitchens for ages.

They needed extra help for a few days at least to care for all those children.

And by all accounts, Elise was very good with old people.

'It's a wonderful reference,' Jill said warmly. 'It's not up to me whether you can have a job but I'll see what I can do. I might not be able to talk to anyone until we've finished seeing our patients. Can you wait for a while?'

'Sure.'

Blow the paperwork.

Escape was definitely in order.

He'd find the woman who'd given him that nice cup of tea and that melt-in-the-mouth home-made shortbread and ask about getting a taxi. Find a motel, maybe. He could always drop in on his way out of town tomorrow and give Jill any details she needed for her database and the government's accident corporation claim forms.

He didn't need to be in hospital but he wasn't stupid enough to be planning a long-distance drive immediately. His headache was bad enough to suggest mild concussion and, anyway, he couldn't take off and leave his pride and joy upside down in a paddock with sheep nibbling the brand-new paintwork. With Ballochburn being the size it was, the cook was bound to know who Wally was and how he could get in touch with him.

But where was she? Having given him the afternoon tea in the kitchen and told him in no uncertain terms he was to sit and take things quietly until further notice, she had sailed off like a battleship with a flotilla of little tugs.

It was about time someone sorted out these poor children, she'd said.

And, no, the dog was not allowed to go upstairs.

The aromatic mutt had gone somewhere, though. Jack was alone in the vast kitchen. His bags were still sitting near the door—a reminder of the nomadic life he'd embarked on. A clear statement that he didn't belong here and it was time to move on. With an effort Jack got to his feet, picked up the bags and left the comforting smell of baking behind.

He'd been down this corridor a couple of times now, on his way to and from the treatment room. He didn't want to bump into Jill or her father so he avoided going left. Looking straight ahead, he could see an atrium-type area with a sweeping staircase and an ancient lift with wrought-iron gates. Presumably the corridor to his right led towards the back door he had entered in the first place but his head felt too fuzzy to remember clearly and this rambling old building was like a rabbit warren.

Cautiously, Jack took an exploratory walk. Between a pair of the tall sash windows were some French doors he hadn't noticed before. They were open and they led onto a veranda and then into the manicured gardens. Somebody was sitting on a bench in the shade of a huge old tree.

Somebody that might know where the battleship woman had gone.

'G'day.'

The boy didn't bother to look up at Jack and he made no response.

'Jarred, isn't it?'

'Yeah.' The admission was reluctant.

Jack sat down on the bench. Even the short walk from the veranda had been enough to make his head pound and the shade was very inviting.

'I'm Jack,' he said politely.

There was no response. Jarred was sitting with his head down. His fingers were buried in the shaggy coat of the smelly dog.

The silence was a little awkward so Jack tried again.

'How's it going?'

'It's not allowed inside. The big lady said so.'

'No.' Jack looked down at the dog. 'I guess that's fair enough. It *is* a hospital.'

'I hate hospitals.'

'So do I, mate.'

'Why do *you* hate them?' It sounded as though it was Jarred's prerogative to hate everything. Jack was encroaching on ground where he wasn't welcome.

'Long story.' Jack leaned back and closed his eyes. 'Do you know where the…ah…big lady is at the moment?'

'She's upstairs with some other ladies. They've found some green stuff for a bath. It's supposed to stop you itching.'

'Right. I guess she's busy, then.'

'She said she'd come down soon. I have to stay here. She sounded cross.'

'I don't think she is cross.' Jack cracked an eyelid half-open. 'She sounded cross when she said I had to stay in the kitchen but I reckon she was just being kind. I'll wait for a bit until she comes down.'

The silence wasn't awkward this time, which was good. What wasn't so good was the feeling of kinship with this kid. Hardly surprising, though, was it? Easy to remember what it was like to be nine years old and feel all alone in the world.

Not that Jarred needed anyone to feel sorry for him. He wasn't really alone. He may have lost his mother but at least she had died and not just gone off because she hadn't wanted him. And he had siblings. A family. And he was going to be looked after by the Metcalfs. To have a Christmas in the parallel universe.

The kind of Christmas a nine-year-old Jack could have only dreamed of.

The kind of fostering that had never come his way—even for a few days.

No. He didn't need to get involved. Or tell the boy any of his own sob story. Jarred was lucky. And it wasn't his problem, anyway.

'What's in the bag?'

'Clothes and stuff.' Jack prodded the back pack with his foot.

'I meant the other bag. The black one.'

'Oh… That's my camera.'

The symbol of his new career. Not that Jack really expected to earn a living from his photographs. He knew it was escapism. What better way to take time out and observe life from a safe distance than to be behind the impersonal lens of a state-of-the-art digital camera?

'Can I see?' Jarred made it sound as though it was of no importance if the request was refused—in fact, he fully expected it to be refused—but Jack remembered that particular defence mechanism only too well.

'If you want,' he said casually. 'I could show you how it works and you could take a picture of Bella.'

The French doors were open.

Jill could hear voices as she hurried towards the kitchen and the deep rumble of one of those voices was already familiar enough to create a warm tingle.

A dangerous but, oh, so delicious tingle.

She paused on the veranda for a moment, caught by the picture in front of her. The two dark heads, close together, with the dappled light from sunshine filtering through leaves creating an almost halo effect.

Bella sat pressed against the boy's leg, her head flat on his lap, looking up with an adoring expression.

Much the same expression as was on Jarred's face when he stole an upward glance at the man sitting beside him. The looking was fleeting, his attention quickly refocussed on the object Jack was holding.

'It's a very good camera,' Jack was saying. 'Lots of professional photographers use it and lots use digital rather than film now. This is the latest model—ten point two mega-pixels.'

'What's a mega-pixel?'

Jill knew she should keep moving and not stand there, eavesdropping, but it was irresistible. Jack sounded different somehow. As though his guard was down. He was also talking to Jarred in a man-to-man fashion and Jill was loath to break into something that was clearly a good distraction from the chaos the boy's life had been plunged into. Heck, it was probably the most exciting thing that had happened to this lad in a long time. She wouldn't pass up the opportunity to have a serious discussion about something—anything, really—with Jack so why should she take it away from someone else?

'A mega-pixel is a measure of how big the CCD is,' Jack said. 'That's the bit of a camera that captures the image. Bottom line is, the more mega-pixels you have, the better quality the picture. You can make it bigger without losing any of the definition.'

'Is ten point two big?'

'Huge.' Jack sounded satisfied. He must love his photography, Jill decided. Was that part of his attraction? A sort of tortured artist quality? 'These pictures are the best you can get.'

'So you could make this one bigger?'

'Yeah. Big as a wall.'

'Can I have one?'

'Sure. Maybe not that big, though. The paper gets awfully expensive. I could make you an ordinary-sized one.'

'When?'

'As soon as I can find a computer to print it out on. I'll post it to you.'

'But I want to show Mel and Jade. And that lady.'

'Well…' Jack was hesitant. Reluctant. 'I guess we could show them on the camera, before I go.'

'When are you going?'

'As soon as I can, mate.'

'Why?' Jarred asked.

Yes, echoed in Jill's head. *Why?* What's the hurry?

'I hate hospitals, remember?'

'Oh…yeah…'

Jill could understand the disappointment in Jarred's voice. More than understand. She could feel it herself. She didn't want Jack to disappear, either.

And he wasn't allowed to. Not just yet.

'Hi,' she said brightly, bouncing down the steps as though she had just emerged in a hurry from the corridor. 'I found you!'

Sitting with his bags by his feet. Looking as though he couldn't wait to escape.

Why did Jack hate hospitals?

And Christmas?

'Jack took my photo.' Jarred sounded nothing like the sullen child she'd left crouching in the corner of the kitchen. 'Me and the dog.'

'Can I see?'

She peered at the screen on the back of the camera and Jack scrolled through several pictures. Some were terrible—just parts of a dog and one of Jack's left foot.

'I took those,' Jarred said proudly.

But then there were several more. Of Jarred and Bella and one in particular made Jill catch her breath. The boy and the dog were looking at each other. Very seriously. There was a kind of amazement caught in that moment. Like a recognition of finding a soul-mate. The very beginning of a love affair.

Jill's heart gave one of those bitter-sweet squeezes. 'That's really lovely,' she whispered. 'I'd like a copy of that one.'

'Sure.' Jack was offhand. Did he not realise the magic he'd captured?

'He can post you one,' Jarred said importantly.

'What sort of computer do you need to print one out on?'

Jack gave her a suspicious glance, as though the possibility she had been eavesdropping had occurred to him. She managed a perfectly innocent smile that said everybody knew about digital cameras.

'Do you need special paper?'

'I've got some paper,' Jack said warily. 'In my bag.'

'We could find a computer, then,' Jill said happily. 'I still need to do that paperwork on you, Jack. There's a good computer in the office.'

'Can I come, too?' Jarred's surly tone was back again. He didn't expect to be included.

'Of course,' Jill said. 'And then we can take your photos up to show the others.'

'Can the dog come?' Still surly. Pushing the boundaries.

'Her name's Bella,' Jill said.

'For now,' Jack put in.

'And she can't come inside a hospital.' Jill tried to sound firm.

'I hate hospitals,' Jarred said. 'So does Jack.'

Jill couldn't help glancing at Jack. He just shrugged. 'They're not usually anyone's favourite place.'

'I'll put her in the gardener's shed for the moment,' Jill decided. 'That way she'll be safe.'

Jarred followed Jill and Bella. 'Does Bella live in the shed?'

'She doesn't live anywhere at the moment. She's a stray.'

Jarred gave a very adult sigh. 'Like me,' he muttered.

Jill put her arm around a skinny set of shoulders and gave him a quick hug. 'Kind of, I guess. She's a bit lost so she needs someone to help look after her for now.'

Jarred's body was stiff. Unresponsive. He pulled away from the hug. They walked in silence for a minute as they headed back to the tree where she could see Jack putting his camera away in the black case.

'I could look after her,' Jarred announced somewhat defensively. 'I like dogs.'

'That would be cool.' Jill tried to sound casual but it was heartbreaking, the longing she could hear beneath the words. Even if it was just a temporary anchor, at least she could offer something to this child. 'You might be able to help me give her a bath later.'

'Mel's having a bath. It's green.'

'That'll be Pinetarsol. It helps stop itching.'

'That's what the lady said.'

'The lady's name is Mrs Drummond,' Jill told Jarred. 'Might be a good idea if you remember that one.'

Jack was watching them now. He had his camera bag over his shoulder, waiting to follow them inside to find the office. He had pushed his backpack under the bench, clearly planning to leave it behind. Jill smiled. This was good. She didn't have to think about his exit from her life just yet.

'Come with me,' she invited. 'Let's go and find that paper-work. And that computer.'

Jack nodded. 'I'll remember Mrs Drummond's name, too,' he said. 'I need to tell her how good her shortbread is.'

'Who were the other ladies?' Jarred enquired. 'Do I need to know their names?'

'That's easy,' Jill told him. 'They're both called Mrs Metcalf.'

'Why do they have the same name?'

'They're in the same family. Like you and Jade and Mel and Nat.' Jill paused. Maybe these children didn't have the same surname, given that they all had different fathers. 'I'm a Metcalf, too,' she added hurriedly. 'Jill Metcalf.'

Jarred thought about that for a moment as the three of them walked along the silent corridor. Then he cast another of those shy glances up at the man walking on his other side.

'That's funny,' he said. 'Isn't it?'

'What is?' Jill responded obligingly.

'Jack and Jill.'

Their gazes caught over the top of Jarred's head.

Jack raised an eyebrow. 'Went up a hill,' he murmured.

Jill grinned. 'Jack fell down and broke his crown. Well, that fits—you got a good bump on the head, anyway.'

He smiled.

Really smiled. The corners of his eyes crinkled and a spark of something gleamed in their dark depths. For just a tiny moment his face came alive.

Jill felt the axis of her world tilt sharply.

And Jill came tumbling after....

She liked him.

He could feel the warmth.

The *giving*.

And it was so seductive. Like the smell of roasting meat to a man who hadn't eaten properly for way too long.

She was just too good to be true, this happy, golden woman.

She would probably give even if she got nothing in return, but that would never be good enough. It would be as bad as being a doctor when you couldn't give a damn about the outcome of any cases you treated.

Jack wished he had something to give.

Anything.

Just enough to let her know that it was good there were people like her in the world. That she was special.

All he had to offer was a smile.

At least she couldn't know how rusty a gift it was.

And, curiously, it seemed to be enough.

CHAPTER FIVE

JUST occasionally, paperwork could transcend being a chore.

It could almost seem exciting.

'Full name?' Jill queried in a brisk, professional manner.

'Jack Sinclair.'

'No middle name?'

'Not that I know of.'

Jill could only frown at Jack's back because he was hunched in front of the computer on the other side of the office, having attached a cable to his camera and slotted shiny paper into the printer. Jarred sat beside him, staring at an image of himself and Bella now filling the screen.

'Cool,' Jarred breathed. He seemed to grow an inch or two as he sat up straighter.

Jill moved on from the unsatisfactory gap on her report form. 'How old are you, Jack?'

'Thirty-three.'

'Home address?'

'Haven't got one.'

'Oh, come on!' This really wasn't good enough. 'You must have an address.'

'Nope.' Jack's tone didn't allow for any further contradiction. 'And I don't have any next-of-kin either, if that's what you're about to ask.'

'Are you an orphan?' Jarred asked.

'Yeah.' The hesitation was noticeable. If Jack Sinclair did have any family, he wasn't about to admit it. Definitely running away from something, Jill decided. Like that girl, Elise, who was probably still sitting in the waiting room, having a life crisis that needed help to sort out. She began scribbling a quick history and treatment summary for Jack.

'I guess I'm an orphan now.' Jill looked up at the quiet words, in time to see Jarred shuffle his chair just an inch or two closer to Jack's.

The mystery man. Jill gave up on the paperwork.

He'd come from nowhere, had no family, hated Christmas and hospitals.

Jill had to resist the urge to go and put her arms around the man. To offer comfort.

Friendship.

Fortunately, she was as distracted as Jarred when the prints started emerging. Jack had made several copies, postcard-sized.

'Hey…thanks!' It was the first time she had seen the boy smile.

'You're welcome.' Jack wound up the cable and tucked it into the camera case. 'I guess I'll be heading off now.'

'No!' The word popped out before Jill could prevent it. 'You can't.'

Jack just raised an eloquent eyebrow and Jill blushed.

'I said you'd come to the Friends of the Hospital meeting tonight,' she offered by way of an explanation.

'The *what*?'

'It's a community group. It got formed years ago when the

hospital was first under threat of closure. It's what's kept us going. They do all sorts of things to cut costs, like the committee that looks after the gardens. And they fundraise. My Aunty Faith is the chairperson.' Jill knew she was babbling but hopefully she was hiding any more personal reasons for not wanting Jack to disappear just yet. 'She does the most. She even provides Christmas dinner for any inpatients and all the staff. It's a real treat.'

Jack had been listening in amazement. Now he was scowling. 'And what on earth does that have to do with me?'

'Wally Briggs is the treasurer of the Friends. He's been to see your plane and I said I'd bring you to the meeting so you could talk to him.'

'What time is the meeting?'

'About 6:30.'

'So I'll come back. I need to find somewhere to stay.'

'There isn't anywhere.'

'There must be.' Jack's tone was an echo of Jill's when he'd failed to provide a home address. 'A pub or motel or cabin in the camping ground or something.'

'Everything's full at this time of year. Even the camping ground. There are waiting lists for people who want to come here for their holidays. They book years in advance sometimes.'

There were empty bedrooms in their parents' house. Rooms that would not be taken up by children needing care.

'I'll go into town and have a look for myself, anyway,' Jack said.

'It's a long walk.'

'I'll get a taxi.'

'We don't have a taxi service.'

'I'll rent a car, then.'

'In Ballochburn? You've got to be kidding.' Jill winced as Jack's scowl deepened. Any second now he would just march out the door and off into the sunset. 'Besides, I want to give you another neurological check before I discharge you.'

'I wasn't aware you'd admitted me.'

'I hadn't.' But Jill smiled thoughtfully. 'That's not a bad idea, though. It would give you somewhere to stay for the night.'

'I'm not staying in a hospital.' Jack emphasised his words by walking towards the office door. Jarred watched, his face empty of expression, the precious photographs clutched in his hand.

Jack's exit was very effectively blocked, however, by the solid form of Maisie Drummond.

'So here you are!' Maisie took in the scene and sighed. 'I've been looking everywhere for you, young man.'

Both Jarred and Jack managed to look guilty.

'It's your turn for a bath,' Maisie pronounced.

Jack looked relieved and earned a frown. 'And Faith wants to talk to you.'

'Who's Faith?' Jarred asked nervously.

'One of the Mrs Metcalfs,' Jill whispered.

'Why does she want to talk to *me*?' Jarred whispered back.

'She doesn't,' Maisie said patiently. Jack was pinned by her stare now. 'She wants to talk to *you*.'

Time was doing odd things in the parallel universe.

This had to have been the longest day in Jack's life and it wasn't even over.

Maybe his perception had been altered by his head injury. That might also explain why he was now in the position he found himself in.

Trapped.

Swept along by a tide he'd had no power to resist.

Faith Metcalf was a force to be reckoned with, that was for sure. When she decided something was going to happen, woe betide anyone who stood in her way.

Jack had tried. 'I'm not the person you need,' he'd said, very firmly. 'And I can't stay.'

'You can't go anywhere. Wally tells me it'll take days to get the parts he needs to fix your plane. Did you realise you had a faulty fuel gauge? That you'd been running on empty?'

'No.' Jack had been horrified. 'The plane's brand-new.'

'Hmmph. Age doesn't necessarily equate to lesser ability to perform, Mr Sinclair.'

'Call me Jack,' he'd said wearily. 'And I'm sorry, but I can't stay. I'm told there's no accommodation available.'

'You can stay right here. For heaven's sake, haven't you noticed how many empty beds there are? There's a whole apartment set up for a locum doctor. You could be perfectly independent.'

'I'm not a locum doctor.' It had been hard to keep the desperation out of his tone.

'You can consider it reimbursement.'

'But I have no experience. I know absolutely nothing about making calendars.'

'What's to know? You can take photographs. Very good photographs.' Faith peered at the picture she was holding of Jarred and Bella and nodded with satisfaction. 'You can capture the spirit of Ballochburn and its hospital. It will be the best fundraiser we've ever managed. We'll be able to afford to attract a permanent doctor.'

'I have to be in Wanaka. Or Queenstown.'

'Why?' Faith was good at making a subtle but exasperated clicking sound with her tongue. 'To capture the spirit of a Kiwi Christmas? You've got it wrong, Mr Sinclair. Those places are far too commercialised now. If you want to capture the genuine article, you've landed in exactly the right place.' Her gaze seemed to penetrate any defences Jack could have mustered. 'And you'll be helping others as well as achieving your own goal.'

How could he refuse without advertising himself as a low-life? A bit of pond scum that didn't give a damn about the rest of humanity?

And if he'd thought his smile had been enough to make Jill happy earlier, it was nothing compared to the joy he saw when she came back from whatever mission she'd taken off on when Maisie had virtually frog-marched him off for his audience with Faith.

'Oh!' Listening to her great-aunt's brilliant plan had made her face positively glow. 'It's *perfect*!'

'No.' Jack's voice was a low growl. 'It's not.'

But Jill had simply ignored the negative noise. 'We've got everything. Cherry orchards and carol singers. Pets' day at school and Christmas dinner and presents. Families camping and barbecues and kids swimming in the river. It's the best place in the world to be for Christmas, Jack. You'll love it.'

No. He wouldn't. He'd be watching the joy of others from behind the lens of a camera. Cut off.

But wasn't that what he'd been planning to do all along?

Yes, but totally anonymously. Not with a nine-year-old boy who was gazing at him with something like hope in his eyes.

Or a golden woman who looked like she was being given the best gift she'd ever had.

Or an ancient matriarch who expected nothing less than compliance, thank you very much.

He should be taking to the hills. Getting as far away from this crazy place as possible. What was it about these people that was exerting a pull Jack felt powerless to fight?

It was more than the sum of the individual personalities, even if he threw in that grumpy cook with the heart of gold, or that large girl she now had in tow as her assistant—Elise. Or Wally, the man with a walrus moustache and a booming voice who was rising to the challenge of an aircraft repair job with military efficiency.

Or Jill's parents. Her mother was clucking over the chickenpox children with obvious contentment. Her father had been seen not long ago stomping off for a walk, muttering that he obviously wasn't needed and nobody was listening to him anyway.

It was more to do with the forest than the trees. The glue that held this community together. Jack could feel his feet sticking to it. He could rationalise his decision to comply with Faith's request by saying he had no means of going anywhere else for a few days but the truth was he didn't want to leave.

Instinct was telling him that fate had brought him there for a purpose. That it was possible he could find what he was looking for right there in Ballochburn.

And now, as the heat and sunshine of this strange day finally faded into a glorious summer dusk, the chorus of birdsong was interrupted only by the peal of laughter coming from outside the apartment window.

The locum doctor's apartment didn't have the best view. It was above the kitchens and its single window looked out not on the gardens but into a courtyard area where there were vehicles parked and a whole bunch of rubbish bins.

But it was the best view.

One that made Jack reach for his camera and position himself, propped against the frame of the open window for stability.

Jill was in the courtyard. Along with Jarred and a large steaming bucket and a stack of what looked like hospital-issue towels. A hose that was running and a dog who was shaking off the foam of the shampoo as fast as the woman and boy could make it lather.

Jill was saturated already. Her hair dangled in damp, curly strands. Her bare feet splashed in the accumulating puddles and her T-shirt stuck to her skin. Jarred held the hose. He fiddled with the nozzle, trying to make it spray. Jill was hanging onto the miserable-looking dog and she was laughing.

The camera shutter clicked and clicked again. It caught the dog shaking a storm of rinse water from its shaggy coat, disappearing under vigorously moving soft towels, emerging to roll ecstatically on the white pebbles and then bark with excitement and go head down, tail up in a puppyish invitation to play.

And it caught a moment that Jack knew was something special even before he scrolled through the collection. A back view of the woman and the boy as they stood admiring the clean dog. As Jill's arm stole around Jarred's shoulders and he'd turned to look up at her…and smile.

Jack may have been cut off by distance and the barrier of his camera. He wasn't an acknowledged part of that scene at all and yet he could feel both sides of that smile. The happiness that had been given to a boy who had far too much of the world's weight on his shoulders.

The happiness of the woman who had, probably unconsciously, given it.

He sat looking at the image for a long time before he tried to sleep that night.

Then he scrolled through the rest of the pictures from Bella's bathtime and it was another image that made him pause, lost in thought.

One of Jill. With her head tilted back as she laughed. With her sopping T-shirt clinging to her body. Cupping her breasts. The quality of the photo was amazing—even her nipples were clearly outlined. Jill wouldn't thank him for a photograph that made her look naked and Jack knew he needed to delete it.

But then he felt it. The curious sinking sensation like an electric shock that originated in his belly and then swooped lower.

Physical attraction.

Not an intellectual appreciation of how attractive Jill Metcalf was.

This was physical.

And *real*.

And it felt like a tiny part of him had sprung back into life.

It didn't matter that it couldn't grow. That he might never be ready to risk hurting himself or others by submitting to involvement. What mattered was that it was there at all. That he was still capable of feeling it.

That he wasn't as emotionally dead as he'd feared.

He could respond to an image. More importantly, he could recognise an image that evoked a response. Not that he would ever use that one of Jill, of course. He deleted it with only a brief flash of regret. The other one of Jill and Jarred was the prize he *could* use.

Maybe he could make this calendar. Capture that glue that made this place magic. Do something that could help others but didn't require any real involvement on his part. He could do that and then just walk away when it was finished.

Jill had been right.

This *was* perfect.

CHAPTER SIX

'GOOD grief! You're doing the dishes!'

Jim didn't turn around from the kitchen bench. 'Don't you start!'

'Start what?' Jill's spirits dropped a notch. Her father didn't sound any happier than he'd been last thing yesterday.

'Going on about how I never do anything to help around the house. I'm perfectly capable of doing whatever *needs* doing.'

'I know that, Dad. It's just a bit of a surprise to find you doing housework at six-thirty in the morning.'

'It's going to be a busy day. I've got patients to see, a mountain of paperwork to do and I'm expected at the school this afternoon to judge a pet rock competition or some such nonsense.'

'Oh, yes, it's pets' day. Cool.' Jill stood on tiptoe to plant a kiss on her father's cheek. 'And I know you love it. You've still got the pet rock I made on your office desk. I saw it yesterday.'

Her father looked tired. Maybe he hadn't slept well, which might explain his early and unusual activity. He looked miserable as well. Clearly he hadn't done anything to try and sort out the impasse with her mother but that was a subject Jill felt she should probably avoid for the moment. Jim's reaction to the news she'd admitted four children with chickenpox and that Hope was helping to care for them in the hospital hadn't exactly helped matters.

'She got what she wanted, then,' Jim had growled. 'Don't know why she bothered asking what I thought in the first place.'

Did her father feel neglected? Like he wasn't as important in Hope's life as the children she helped? Did her mother feel taken for granted? Like she was only important as a house-keeper? Had her parents become so caught up in their own interests they had just gradually drifted apart?

No. Jill refused to believe this was anything more than a minor disturbance. And she had a feeling Aunty Faith was right in saying it was something they had to sort out for themselves. She shouldn't interfere so she couldn't help feeling a trifle guilty at the unspoken accusation that she had taken sides by aiding and abetting her mother as far as the homeless children were concerned. It created tension that was unsettling.

'I'm going to take Bella for a quick walk before breakfast,' she said. 'And then I'll get on with a ward round.'

'Good. You admitted all those children so they can be your responsibility as well.'

'Of course.'

'Keep an eye on them. People think chickenpox is just another run-of-the-mill childhood illness like an ear infection or a cold, but you can get some nasty complications.'

'I know. Secondary bacterial infection of the skin lesions, cerebellitis, transverse myelitis, even pneumonitis or enceph-alitis in patients with abnormal T-cell immunity.'

Her father finally smiled. 'I'm glad to see you paid atten-tion at medical school.'

'Anything else you want me to put on my list for the morning?'

'If you can. Sue couldn't make it in to pick up that morphine yesterday. I told her one of us would drop it out.'

'I should be able to fit that in.' Jill nodded. 'In fact, I'd love to. I've been trying to get out to see them for days and I was planning to take Jack. He needs to visit a cherry orchard to get some photos for Aunty's calendar.'

'Bloody calendar,' Jim muttered. 'Where does she get her ideas from?'

'I think it'll be great.'

'I can't say I approve of that plane-crash fellow staying in the doctor's accommodation either. What if I get a new locum turning up?'

'Hardly likely, this close to Christmas, but if we do, Jack can come and stay with us.'

'Ah, yes…' Jim dried his hands on a teatowel. 'The Metcalf Motel. Free to anyone who needs a bed.'

'It's only for a few days, Dad. This isn't like you. Where's your Christmas spirit?'

'Gone west,' he said gloomily. 'Like your mother seems to have.'

'Where did you say we were going?'

'To the Wheelers' orchard. Dave might not be there. He's probably at school with the boys for pets' day. The orchard manager won't mind if you take pictures, but they'll be very busy getting the final Christmas orders picked and packed. There'll be teams picking outside and probably chaos in the packing sheds. Very Christmassy.'

'The chaos or the cherries?'

'Both. I can never see a bowl of cherries without thinking of Christmas. And the chaos is part of the fun, isn't it?'

'If you say so.'

'And it's very Ballochburn—cherries. Along with peaches and apricots, of course. And apples in winter.'

'Nice healthy place.'

'Mmm.' Jill couldn't help her ironic tone. 'I could wish it was a bit healthier right now.'

'Why?'

'This house call I'm making. I'm dropping off a supply of morphine for a terminally ill patient.'

'Oh…'

It wasn't her imagination. Both the tone and the way her passenger visibly stiffened in his seat suggested discomfort. He didn't want to know.

Well, tough! If Jack was going to get into the real spirit of her home town, maybe there were some things he needed to know.

'Sue Wheeler is my oldest friend,' Jill told him. 'The only one left in Ballochburn, at any rate. We went right though school together but she never wanted to escape like the rest of us. She fell in love with Dave at high school and all she ever wanted was to live on his family's orchard and raise a family. They got married at nineteen and Sue was already pregnant.'

They were on the road that led past Faith's cottage now but Jill barely spared a glance for the eye-catching rosebush hedge.

'They had three little boys in the space of four years. The oldest one is nearly ten but Sue always wanted a daughter so they tried one more time and they had Emma almost three years ago. They were so happy.' Jill sighed. 'And then it all turned into a bit of a nightmare eighteen months ago.'

'She got sick?'

'Yeah. Nothing specific to start with, but Sue just knew something wasn't right. Dad listened, as he always does, and he went the extra mile to try and find what was wrong. They couldn't have diagnosed the cancer any earlier but it wasn't enough to save her.'

'What sort of cancer?'

'Abdominal. Something incredibly rare. Sue blamed herself for a while. She thought maybe it had something to do with the sprays they use in the orchards but there's no evidence. It's just one of those tragic stories.'

'How long has she got?'

'Not long. The family's hoping to have this last Christmas together. She's not in too much pain and there's any amount of support from the community for them all. It's wonderful that she *can* be at home. It's just really, really sad.'

'Yeah…' Jack was staring through the side window. Jill could almost see the barrier he'd erected around himself.

It was disappointing that the story hadn't touched him but, then, he didn't know these people, did he? If you took on board the sadness of every stranger that crossed your path, it would drag anybody down.

Jill stole another glance at Jack a moment later, however. It wasn't enough of a reason. Had she imagined the glimpses of warmth she had seen in this man?

Like when he had smiled at her over the amusement of being 'Jack and Jill'?

Or when she had seen him, shoulder to shoulder with Jarred, giving him the self-esteem of being talked to man to man?

Had she seen those glimpses because she had been looking for them? Hoping to find them because it would give a depth to her attraction to him and make it more meaningful than something purely physical?

Perhaps it would be just as well to be proved wrong. It

would make it easier when Jack picked up his bags and disappeared from her life.

He was still staring out of his window.

'Don't worry,' Jill said a little flatly. 'You don't have to come into the house. I'll be half an hour or so. You can get some pictures in the orchard and stuff.'

They were only a few minutes from the Wheelers' orchard when Jill's pager sounded.

'It's a PRIME page,' she said aloud, pulling the Jeep onto the wide grass verge. 'I need to call the emergency services control centre and see why I'm needed.'

'The Jefferson orchard?' she said moments later. 'Yes, I know where it is. I'm actually just down the road.'

She finished the call, pulled the Jeep into a U-turn and picked up speed rapidly.

'It's an accident,' she informed Jack. 'The neighbouring orchard to the Wheelers' which is a bit lucky. Someone's fallen from a cherry picker.'

Jack had to catch hold of the doorhandle as Jill put her foot on the brake and then turned onto a shingle road with a skid of tyres. Bella fell over in the back with a thump.

'Whoops! Sorry, Bella.' But Jack caught the flash of a smile. She was enjoying the adrenaline rush of an emergency response.

Jack wasn't. He would rather not be feeling it at all but he couldn't stop it, any more than the automatic action of leaping out of the vehicle as soon as it came to an abrupt halt by the waving figure of the orchard manager.

Or scanning the area, to see the empty basket of a cherry picker several metres from the ground. The supine figure beneath it and the group of shocked-looking young people standing around.

Jill's gaze had swept the scene, making the same assessment. Now she focussed on the man who'd met their vehicle.

'So he fell from that basket?'

'Yes.'

'Was he knocked out?'

'Yeah, he landed on his head.'

'Is he conscious now?'

'Yes.'

'Nobody's tried to move him, have they?'

'No.'

'That's good.'

Jack agreed silently. Given the mechanism of injury and the way the lad had landed, a spinal injury had to be very high on the list of suspected trauma. The inclination to step in and take over—to make sure any injury wasn't exacerbated by incorrect handling—was strong.

Too strong.

Jack had to remind himself he'd given up the practice of medicine, at least for the time being. It wasn't as though his skills were needed. Jill was the doctor here. And as far as she knew, he was simply a photographer. What would she think if he told her the truth?

She'd think she had been deceived, that's what. That he was an untrustworthy person. Jack didn't want Jill's opinion of him to lessen. He clamped his mouth shut. He stayed where he was beside the Jeep as Jill hoisted the pack from the back and moved off towards the victim.

But then she looked over her shoulder.

'Jack? Could you come, too, please? I might need a hand.'

She crouched beside their patient a moment later. 'Hey,' she said. 'I'm Jill Metcalf. I'm a doctor.' She took hold of the youth's wrist, feeling for his pulse.

It was the same introduction she had used with *him* yesterday. When he had been sitting in that sheep paddock, feeling like he'd stepped from one disaster in his life straight into another. Jack could remember that touch, too. The connection with another human that he hadn't wanted because it had carried an obligation. You shouldn't accept something when you had nothing to give in return.

'What's your name?' Jill asked.

'Nick.'

'How old are you, Nick?'

'Eighteen.'

'Can you remember what happened?'

'It was an accident.' One of the teenagers standing nearby was white-faced. 'I didn't think it was going to move that fast and I didn't know Nick was leaning out so far.'

Jill was gently moving Nick's head and neck into a neutral position. 'Jack? Could you come here and hold Nick's head? It's very important that it's kept still.'

'Sure.' Jack knelt by Nick's head. He knew exactly what he needed to do but he let Jill take his hands to position them, palms against Nick's cheeks, his fingers supporting his chin, his thumbs cradling the back of the skull.

'Does anything hurt, Nick?'

'Yeah… My back…and my neck.'

Jack's fingers stiffened a little as he concentrated. His support could be crucial right now.

Jill continued her questioning. 'Are you having any trouble breathing?'

'I…don't think so but I…can't move my legs.'

'Can you squeeze my hands?' Jill frowned slightly after she slipped her hands into Nick's. 'Harder?'

'I've got, like, pins and needles in my fingers.'

The indications were certainly there for a serious spinal injury. Jack could almost see the wheels turning in Jill's mind. He wanted to help. To make sure nothing was forgotten. A collar, a bag mask nearby in case assistance was needed if Nick's breathing became affected. Back-up that could provide the board and foam cushions and body straps needed for complete immobilisation. Baseline vital signs. IV access. He wanted to know if rural protocols allowed for a loading dose of steroids that could reduce the damage from inflammation of the spinal cord.

But Jill clearly didn't need his input and she certainly wasn't expecting it. The same kind of list had to be running through her head and she was acting on every thought. She knew what she was doing, too. The neck collar was positioned with the utmost care and strapped into place.

'I still need you to hold his head, Jack. You're doing a fantastic job.'

The brief smile she gave him was very different to the impish grin he was getting used to, but it included him in this incident and made him feel appreciated.

The smile and reassuring words she had for Nick were more than just professional. They held a sincerity and warmth that Jack knew was as important for this terrified young man as any medical intervention.

'You've hurt your back,' Jill told him honestly, 'but we can't know how serious it is yet. What we need to do is look after you very carefully and get you to the experts. I'm going to see if a rescue helicopter is available rather than try and move you by ambulance. Where's home for you?'

'Dunedin. I'm at varsity there.'

'We'll try and make that the first stop, then.' She moved away a little to make a call on her mobile phone but snatches of the conversation floated back to Jack.

'Paralysis, both legs… Paraesthesia, both arms… KO'd but GCS is now 15…'

An ambulance pulled up a few minutes later as Jill deftly slid an intravenous cannula into place in Nick's forearm. A middle-aged man climbed from the emergency vehicle as she finished taping the line securely and began setting up a bag of saline.

'Hi, Ted,' she called. 'Could you grab an oxygen cylinder for me, please?'

Jill handed the bag of fluid to one of Nick's friends to hold and adjusted the flow of the fluid to no more than a slow drip that would just keep a vein open. Jack nodded inwardly. The low blood pressure of 80 systolic she had already recorded on Nick was probably due to vasodilation caused by the shock of the injury. If she pumped fluids in to try and raise the pressure to a normal 100 instead of 80, she could risk complications from over-hydration. He was also pleased to note her care in administering pain relief. The potential effects on breathing from narcotics was something that needed experienced monitoring.

'I'm cold,' Nick said.

'Want a foil sheet?' The ambulance officer asked Jill.

'Yes, please, Ted. And the life pack. And a small towel. I want to roll it up to protect the neck lordosis.'

'Scoop stretcher?'

'No. We've got a chopper on the way and they'll have their

own gear. I might just use your radio and see if they can put me in contact with the pilot. I'll find out how far away they are.'

She did more than that. Jack listened to her giving the precise GPS co-ordinates for the orchard after checking a notebook she had taken from her pack. She chose a suitable landing site at one side of the packing shed that had no obstacles like power lines and, having finished the call, she directed some of the young bystanders to shift vehicles and check to make sure no loose debris was in the vicinity that could get sucked up into the helicopter rotors.

Her orders were concise and firm. Nobody was going to argue with anything she said. Including Jack. There was nothing he could have been doing to improve the management of this case.

To say he was impressed was an understatement.

His first impression of Jill Metcalf had been of a Christmas angel masquerading as a medic. But this was an angel with attitude. No wonder she loved working in an emergency department. Performing under pressure.

The noisy arrival of a large helicopter and the fierce blast of air from its rotors only a short distance away might have seriously ruffled Jill's shoulder-length curls but it did nothing to her level of calm assurance.

Her handover managed to convey everything the paramedics needed to know without alarming Nick. She continued to reassure him as she helped to immobilise him onto the backboard.

'These guys are the best,' she told him, 'and they'll be able to give you something more for the pain as well.' Her glance caught the flight crew leader. 'I've got morphine drawn up but he's only had 5 milligrams so far. I'd rather wait till you've got him hooked up to your monitors before giving him any more.'

She went with them as far as the helicopter to help load their patient. Jack made himself useful by tidying up the medical kit and putting it back in the Jeep. He nodded at Bella, who was sitting on his seat and hadn't tried to get out of the open door.

'You're a good dog,' he told her. 'Thank you for looking after my camera.'

A glance upward showed him that preparations for take-off were almost complete. The doors were shut, Jill had run back from the makeshift landing site and the rotors were picking up speed again.

Jack reached for the black bag on impulse and took his camera out. He was just in time to get a brilliant photograph as the rescue helicopter took off.

The force of the air from the rotors flattened the leaves on the cherry trees, exposing bunches of fruit as glossy and red as the paintwork on the chopper.

The group of young workers stood together, some with their arms around each other, watching the helicopter take off, concern for their friend in their faces.

Jill and the ambulance officer, Ted, were in the shot as well, also looking upwards, but their expressions suggested satisfaction in a job well done and hope that the outcome would be good.

If Faith wanted a picture that spoke of the vital role the town's doctor and volunteer ambulance service played in this remote community, this would be a winner.

Surprisingly, Jill seemed a lot less than satisfied as they got back into the Jeep to carry on with the original house call they had been diverted from.

'I'd rather be at the other end,' she confessed. 'With things like X-rays and CT scans on tap. With a neurosurgeon to call in and a theatre and intensive care unit in the same building.'

'Perhaps what happens on scene like that is just as important as far as the final outcome goes.'

Jill gave him a surprised glance. 'Gosh, you sound just like my dad. And it's true, I guess—for any major trauma in an isolated place. I suppose I'll just have do what Dad does and ring the hospital later to follow up.' Then she smiled. 'I do like helicopters, I must admit. You don't get a bit of excitement like that in any emergency department.'

There was no point trying to take pictures at the Wheelers' orchard. Having heard about the accident next door, the workers were subdued. Doing their jobs because the work had to be done. Or maybe the atmosphere was a little grim because of what was going on in the homestead that swallowed Jill up for at least thirty minutes.

A home that should have excited children preparing for Christmas, not facing the loss of their mother.

No wonder Jill look even more subdued than the workers when she finally emerged and put her kit back in the vehicle. She said nothing as they drove away and the silence continued until Jack began to feel uncomfortable.

Something needed to be said. Not that Jack had any desire to get involved, but it was a worry. He may not have known Jill for very long but he knew that it was wrong for her to look this deflated.

Even Bella sensed something wrong. She poked her head between the seats and gazed up at their driver.

Finally, Jack couldn't stand it any longer. He gritted his teeth.

'Are you OK?' The rhetorical question was gruff.

'No.'

The gears crunched roughly as Jill pulled off the road a few seconds later into a deserted rest area. There was a wooden table with built-in bench seats and a three-sided concrete box with a blackened interior that had been used for many a barbecue. The Jeep bumped past the table and down a steep track through trees and Jack caught his first glimpse of Ballochburn's river.

It was a typical New Zealand braided river, with both deep and shallow channels running past shingle islands. At some distance downstream he could see people. Faint shouts of glee and splashing reached them from youngsters who were jumping from a rock ledge into a deep swimming hole. High-school students on holiday, perhaps. It could be a good place to get photographs.

Later.

He couldn't suggest it, though. Not when Jill was sitting, gripping the steering-wheel with white knuckles even after she had brought the vehicle to a standstill.

To Jack's horror, tears were rolling down her cheeks.

He could understand her pain. She had to be so involved with a patient who was also a dear friend. She had to deal with feeling impotent, as if all the years of training and accumulated knowledge was useless.

No point in reminding her of her own blithe statement that you could deal with the downside of this career by focussing on the good stuff. He knew better than anything how inadequate that could be. He also knew the depths of despair it could pull you into and he didn't want to go there again because of Jill's unhappiness.

But he couldn't sit there and do nothing. He could feel her pain and as much as he didn't want to get involved, he already was simply by being there.

Awkwardly, he touched her arm, trying to convey at least the comfort of companionship.

'I'm sorry,' he said, his voice still gruff. Reluctant. Somehow his hand trailed down her arm and he felt his fingers being gripped. They were holding hands. Or rather Jill was holding *his* hand. Tightly enough to make it impossible to pull away.

'I'll be OK.' She sniffed wetly. 'Sorry. I just need a minute to pull myself together.'

She could do that? How?

'It's beautiful, really,' Jill said a few moments later. 'It's just Sue and Emma in there cuddled up, watching cartoons. Emma just adores them. They've set up a bed for her in the living room and they have videos running almost twenty-four hours a day for her.'

'Emma?' Jack felt something cold and nasty slide down his spine. Involuntarily, his fingers tightened around Jill's. 'It's *Emma* who's dying?'

Jill nodded. She sniffed again and scrubbed her nose with the base of her thumb. 'Where's a tissue when you really need one?' she asked with a watery smile.

Jack didn't even try to smile back. 'The little girl?' he queried slowly. 'The daughter your friend wanted so much?'

Jill nodded again. 'She's gorgeous. I've got to know her pretty well this year because they were in Auckland for months. They've been to the best paediatric specialists in the country over the last eighteen months. Everything that could have been tried has been tried but they can't stop the cancer. The tumour's the biggest part of her now and it hurts to move her, but as long as she's still and she has her family around her, she's actually happy.' Another tear escaped but got brushed firmly away. 'She's got the most incredible smile, Jack. Everyone who meets Emma just falls in love with her. And everyone is making the most of every moment she's still with us.'

Jack was transfixed. Still holding her hand. Searching Jill's face as though he expected to find something he was looking for. It wasn't that he felt drawn into the tragedy of the little girl. He felt nothing but an intellectual appreciation of how sad it was.

He couldn't get involved.

But Jill could. She was in it up to her eyebrows. She must know how to cope.

'How can you do it?' he asked quietly. 'Be so involved— as a friend *and* a doctor—knowing what has to come?'

'It's part of what medicine is all about,' she answered. 'It's one of those jobs that is a lot more than a career, you know? I suppose it defines who you are as much as *what* you are.'

Jill took a deep breath and blinked hard, several times. She stared through the windscreen at a river she probably wasn't seeing.

'I think it's a relationship as much as a job. It takes over your life and sometimes it can interfere with other relationships. I think that might be what's going on with my parents at the moment. But Dad has to give as much as he does to his work. That's who he is. Who *I* am, too.' She paused and swallowed. Jack could see the movement of her throat. Could sense her gathering her thoughts.

'It's like any other relationship,' she continued softly. It was almost as though he wasn't there and she was just thinking aloud. 'You get back only as much as you're prepared to give.

If you don't feel the pain of cases you can't help—like wee Emma—you can't feel the joy of all the cases you can help.'

Jack said nothing. In a parallel universe that was probably true. It hadn't worked where he'd come from, though, had it?

'The joy nurtures you,' Jill said finally. 'It gives you strength to deal with the other bits.'

'And that's enough?'

'Not always. The bad bits suck.' Her smile was stronger now. 'Like now. This is the kind of time I need the people who care about me. Like my family.' She eased her hand from Jack's as though she knew he wasn't one of those people. His hand felt cold. Empty. He reached back and scratched Bella's ear in the hope of erasing the emptiness, but it didn't quite work.

Was that why he hadn't coped? Because he'd never had a family? But he had stopped needing one long ago. When he had been about Jarred's age, in fact, and had known that he had to rely on himself to survive.

Jill was looking at the river now. Seeing it. She watched the children in the distance for a moment. 'It's my rock, this place,' she told Jack. 'It's where I get my strength. If I'm lucky enough to find a life partner, I might be able to cut the umbilical cord but until then my heart is here.' She gave a final sniff then started the engine. 'Sorry. I didn't mean to get so heavy. It's probably the last thing you need.'

Jack shook his head but Jill was reversing and didn't see. He wanted to say something to reassure her. Even to say that it might be exactly what he *did* need, but his mouth refused to cooperate.

Something held him back from saying anything because he knew if he started, he might not be able to stop. To tell Jill everything would mean opening a door he had spent the last months trying to close. And lock. Suddenly he was feeling confused. As though he had just realised he must have taken a wrong turning but had no idea how to get himself back to the last signpost. If there had even *been* a signpost.

The opportunity passed before he had any chance of weighing up whether or not to grasp it. They were driving on the road again and Jill had, indeed, pulled herself together.

She was looking forward, not back.

'The pets' day parade is at two o'clock. We'll need to try and get there a bit earlier than that so you can get some good photos. We'll have to hope there aren't any more emergency callouts but if there are, I'll leave you at the school and go by myself.'

Jack had to share the hope there wouldn't be another callout.

What if Jill ended up sitting beside a river and crying all by herself?

With no one to hold her hand?

She'd cope, he reminded himself. Angels with attitude could cope with anything. It wasn't as if he was going to be around for long. Jill wasn't even going to be around for that long. She'd be off, heading for a brilliant career as an emergency physician. She'd find a partner for life with no difficulty whatsoever.

Jack was left wondering how someone who could have been lucky enough to have won Jill—married her, in fact— had managed to mess it up. Had he not recognised how incredibly special this woman was?

CHAPTER SEVEN

BALLOCHBURN school's playing field was awash with colour.

Crowded with people that represented a large proportion of the community. Babies in front packs and pushchairs, proud grandparents wielding cameras, equally proud but somewhat anxious parents. And children. Dozens of children and their pets.

Ponies, calves, lambs, dogs, cats, even hens and an alpaca were being led, carried, positioned or played with. The sound of the children calling to each other, scolding their pets, laughter and the occasional wail of a baby made a cacophony of sound that took Jill back in time instantly.

So did the smell, where frying sausages and onions were competing fairly successfully with the more earthy aroma the pets were providing.

'I haven't been to a pets' day since I was twelve years old,' she told Jack.

'Looks like a circus.'

'Yeah,' Jill agreed happily. 'Isn't it great?' She attached a lead to Bella's new collar and anchored her to the towbar of the Jeep. 'People will be able to see you here,' she told the dog. 'Who knows? Someone might know where you belong.'

Jack took another glance over his shoulder as they walked into the school playground. 'I think she's decided she belongs to you.'

'I can't keep her.' Jill resisted the urge to look back. She knew Bella would be staring longingly in her direction. 'I'm not going to be here very long and I could hardly take her with me to Melbourne, could I?'

'I guess not.' Jack lifted the camera that was hanging around his neck and began taking pictures.

Jill was happy to keep pace with her companion, pausing frequently, just soaking up the atmosphere as they got closer to the action.

Good times.

If strength could be found in happy memories then the traditional country celebration of school pets' day was exactly what Jill needed today. It marked the end of the school year. The beginning of the long summer holiday and it was easy to remember how endlessly it had stretched ahead of her as a child. So full of sunshine and the promise of good things.

Not that she was feeling anything like as bad as she had just after the visit to the Wheelers that morning. It should be embarrassing that she'd cried all over Jack's shoulder but, curiously, it wasn't. It didn't matter if she saw her at her worst, did it? In a couple of days he would be gone and probably wouldn't even remember her. Just as well he had no idea how drawn to him she was. How comforting she had found his presence.

How right it had felt to be holding his hand while she'd spilled out her grief. Weird that she could feel this close to a stranger.

Being a family celebration, it seemed only proper that all the Metcalfs were in attendance. Making a slow circuit around the playground, Jill spotted the classroom set aside for displaying the sand saucers. Hope was in there, judging the miniature gardens that had been made by using flowers, leaves, small toys and lots of imagination. Jack looked amazed at the creations when Jill took him inside and he began snapping photographs.

'Hi, Mum. Did you bring Jarred to help you?'

'He'd never heard of a pets' day. I thought it would be nice for him to have an outing.' Hope sounded a little defensive. 'You did say he wasn't infectious any more.'

'I think it's a great idea. Are you enjoying it, Jarred?'

The boy dragged his gaze from where Jack was leaning over a desk, getting a close-up shot of a tiny farm scene in a saucer, where leaves were trees and tiny plastic sheep grazed beside a lurid-looking pond made from a toffee wrapper.

'It's OK,' he said. 'Where's Bella? I thought you were going to bring her. That's why we gave her a bath, wasn't it?'

'She's tied up to the Jeep, which is parked under an oak tree near the bike sheds. You can take her for a walk later, if you want.'

'We won't be staying too long,' Hope said. 'I just came to judge the sand saucers. I told Jade and Mel I'd take some sausages back for them.'

'Who's looking after them at the moment?'

'That new girl that Maisie's training up. Elise. She's marvelous with young children. She's been helping in the wards with the oldies as well. And in the kitchens. I suspect she's a treasure.'

Moving on, they found Jill's father in the neighbouring classroom, trying to grade pet rocks, some of which were quite large samples of river stones painted to look like animals.

'Oh, I love the hedgehog!' Jill grinned at the round stone

that had had long tree thorns superglued all over it. 'Wish I'd thought of that.'

There were sleeping cats, mice, birds and quite a few rocks that had just been painted bright colours and given faces. Jack went around the room with her but had to stop when a small girl tugged on his elbow.

'It's fallen off,' she said with a wobbly lip. 'Can you help me, mister?'

'What's fallen off?'

'Spot's bow.'

Spot appeared to be a shapeless stone that had felt ears glued on the top and a blob of black paint for a nose. The tartan ribbon that had created the impression of a neck was in the girl's hand.

Jill watched, fascinated, as Jack tried to reattach the bow. He was fumbling but she didn't want to offer to help. The care he was taking, and the automatic way he'd responded to a child's plea, had captured her. The threat of tears had receded completely. The girl was beaming at Jack's efforts.

She hadn't been wrong about his warmth. Behind those barriers lurked a very *nice* man.

Jill needed to turn away then. To pretend she was absorbed with the artistic endeavours on display.

'These are wonderful. Rather you than me, picking the best, Dad. And have you seen the sand saucers? They're amazing, too.'

'No,' her father said shortly. 'I haven't.'

At least her parents were in separate classrooms, Jill thought. Faith was probably the only other person present who would realise that Jim and Hope still weren't talking to each other.

Her great-aunt appeared as calm and dignified as ever. Jill spotted her as soon as they left the pet rocks behind and headed for the grass of the playing field. In a silk dress, with her wide-brimmed hat and an ebony cane that was her only concession to advanced age, Faith was in the company of Bruce Mandeville, carefully inspecting a long row of pet lambs.

'Dr Jill! Over here!'

'Hey, Aaron! How's the arm?'

'Getting better. We gave Rambo a bath. Come and smell him.'

Jill obligingly crouched and buried her nose in soft white wool. 'Mmm. He smells like passionfruit.'

'My conditioner,' Aaron's mother said wryly. 'A whole bottle of it, no less.'

There were so many animals to admire. So many people who wanted to say hello.

'Jilly! Haven't seen you for far too long. How are you?'

'I'm fine, Don. And you? How's the hip?'

'Better than new. I'm glad your dad talked me into having that operation. I can almost keep up with the grandkids now.'

And only a minute later, 'Jillian! Is that really you, dear?'

'Sure is, Miss Reynolds. Aren't you glad I haven't brought a pet lamb this year?'

'At least you cleaned up the mess it made.' The grey-haired teacher was eager to hug her former pupil. 'I've been keeping up with your news through Hope.'

'You're still in the choir, then?'

'Oh, yes. We'll be at the hospital tonight for the carol service. Is it true you've got a job at Melbourne's biggest hospital?'

'It is.'

'And you fought off hundreds of other applicants? Congratulations, dear.'

'I'm sure my parents have been exaggerating.' This *was* embarrassing, to have Jack overhear such admiration. 'It is an amazing job to be going to, though.'

'Well deserved, my dear. I always knew you were going to turn out to be something rather special.'

Jack didn't appear to be listening to the fulsome praise. He was taking a photograph of Aaron proudly holding the red satin sash designating first place over Rambo's head while trying to stand on the rope to anchor his pet. It wasn't hard for the large lamb to pull free. Aaron fell over backwards and for the first time Jill heard Jack laugh aloud.

'Fantastic,' he said. 'What a shot!'

'Ow!' Aaron wailed. 'Rambo, come back!'

'Go and chase him,' his mother ordered. 'Quick!'

'You must know everybody here,' Jack commented as they watched Aaron chasing his pet, the red ribbon fluttering from his fist.

'Just about.'

'Everybody seems to know everybody.'

'It's a small community.'

'More like a big family.'

'I guess. It's not always this rosy a picture, though. We get our fair share of upsets.'

'Like a family,' Jack repeated. 'It must have been hard to leave.'

'Not really. I had no choice. I had to grow up and leave home. I did my last couple of years at a boarding school in Dunedin. That made it easier.'

'But you said your heart's here. Don't you want to come back?'

'Not to live. I couldn't.'

'Why not?'

'I'd always wanted to be a doctor. I just grew up knowing that's what I'd be. Like my dad.'

'Being here hasn't stopped him practising medicine.'

'It's different for a woman. I couldn't practise here, even if I wanted to.'

'Why not?' Jack asked again.

'You remember what I was talking about this morning? About medicine being a kind of relationship?'

'I'm not likely to forget.'

'Oh…' Jill bit her lip. 'Sorry. You seem to be a bit too easy to talk to.' She looked away, at the parade lines that were now forming. If Jack didn't want to talk on a personal level any more, that was fine.

'I'm not complaining,' he said. He had raised his camera and was taking shots. 'Talk away.'

'Well, it's not the only relationship I want in my life, you know?'

'So you said.' Jack turned from the camera for a moment and raised an eyebrow. 'Good for you. A lot of people are put off when they've been badly hurt by a relationship that's gone wrong.'

For a minute they watched the parade in silence. Children rode past on their ponies, others dragged reluctant lambs and one boy was stuck with a calf that was firmly refusing to move. Jill's curiosity got the better of her and she interrupted the photographic session.

'How do you know I was badly hurt?'

'How long ago did your marriage end?'

'More than two years. My divorce is all finalised.'

'And when did you take your wedding ring off?'

'Oh…' Jill looked down at the third finger of her left hand. The pale mark where her ring had been was pretty obvious, wasn't it? 'Yeah, I guess it did take awhile to come to terms with it. I finally took it off as a kind of symbol of leaving my old life behind. I had kept it on so long as a kind of warning, I think. To remind myself to look before I leap. Not to trust so easily or completely. I was really naïve.'

'And you're not now?'

'No.' Jill shook her head confidently. 'I know what I'm looking for and I'd never be able to find it in Ballochburn.'

Jack didn't have to ask why not again. It was written on his face.

'I'd be marrying a sheep farmer or an orchardist if I stayed here,' she elaborated. 'They'd have to understand and deal with the kind of commitment it takes to be a good doctor. The time involved and the way it can interfere with family life. Especially somewhere like here, where there's no after-hours service and you're practically permanently on call.'

'Your parents made it work.'

'Did they? I'm beginning to wonder if that's a big part of what's wrong at the moment. They've drifted apart. How much has that got to do with the practice?'

'But you were married to a doctor before and that didn't work.'

Jill was silent for a moment but her response came easily enough to surprise her. 'He was only a doctor on the outside. At a deep level he cared about himself more than anyone else. I can't operate that way. If nothing else, the failure of my marriage has shown me how important that caring is. I think it's a gift. Like being able to paint or sing or—' she smiled at Jack '—to take great photographs.'

'But doctors are more likely to have it?'

'No, of course not. But maybe people who have it are more likely to go into careers that are people-oriented. Caring professions.'

'So a sheep farmer or orchardist might well have what you're looking for. You shouldn't write them all off.'

'That's true.' Jill's grin was mischievous. Deliberately lightening the conversation. 'OK, maybe there just isn't anyone in Ballochburn that I fancy the socks off. Oh, look!'

Jarred had Bella in tow. They had gravitated to where the dogs were being judged before they joined the end of the parade. Miss Reynolds was handing out the prizes. A red ribbon went to a girl who had a small fluffy white dog that had a Christmas decoration attached to its head.

'I have an extra ribbon,' Jill heard her old teacher announce as they drew nearer. 'I think it should be for a special visitor. Jarred, isn't it?'

Jarred ducked his head shyly but another boy gave him a nudge with his elbow.

'Go on—it's just a ribbon and your dog's cool.'

It wasn't just a ribbon, though. Jill could see the way it was still clutched in his fist after he'd taken part in the small parade around the playground. Like the way he had held onto that photograph Jack had taken of him. She could also see the longing gaze he gave the other boys when Hope came to tell him she had finished judging sand saucers and it was time to go.

'Leave him with us, Mum,' Jill said. 'We'll bring him back later.'

They joined the queue for sausages wrapped up in bread with lashings of tomato sauce. They watched the races start after lunch when parents joined in with their children for sack and egg-and-spoon races.

'Do you think I could go in one?' Jarred finally asked.

'I'm sure you could,' Jill answered. 'Let's go and ask Miss Reynolds.'

The only race left was a three-legged one where children had to be paired with an adult.

'I could do it with you,' Jill offered.

Jarred shook his head slowly. His gaze slid sideways—towards Jack.

'I need to take photos,' Jack said apologetically.

'I could take a photo of this one,' Jill suggested. 'But have you ever been in a three-legged race?'

Jack looked at Jarred and the hesitation was so slight she was probably the only one to notice.

'Sure I have,' he said.

The white lie was obvious from the first step they tried to take with their inside legs bound together with an old rugby sock. They were out of step and fell over in a tumble of mismatched limbs. Jill could see the agony of mortification on Jarred's face.

Then she saw the way Jack helped him up and put his arm around the boy and she felt something melt inside her. She completely forgot to take any photographs, watching the moments he took to figure out how to make the race work and explain it to Jarred. Tentatively, they tried again and took a successful step. And then another. They picked up speed but it was way too late and they were last by such a big margin that they got a bigger clap than the winners. And they both looked even more delighted than the winners had.

It really was time to go after that and it became something

of a rush as Jill realised she was late to help her father with the general practice clinic due to run from 4 p.m. till 7 p.m. The hassle of putting up the extra seat in the back of the Jeep so that Jarred had a safety belt was a nuisance but Jill declined Jack's offer of assistance other than to move the medical gear out of the way.

'It's tricky but I know how to do it,' she told him. 'I have to release this clip here and hold it up and the rest kind of flips open.'

Like an extra-strong deckchair. The seat folded out and then the metal bar that provided its support flipped down to lock into the catch on the floor. It folded easily enough. The bar sprang open with alacrity. Unfortunately, Jill let it go a moment before it reached the catch and the mechanism snapped shut again. Even more unfortunately, Jill had her hand in exactly the wrong place and the fingers of her right hand got crushed between the two bars.

She gasped with shock.

'Oh, no!' Jack dropped the pack he was still holding and wrenched the bars apart. 'Are you hurt?'

'Um…' Jill stared at her hand. Her middle finger had an odd dent around midway between the knuckle and the joint and the whole finger was white. Then the pain message finally reached her brain and instinctively she put her uninjured hand over the other and cradled it to her chest.

'Let me see,' Jack demanded. He lifted her hand away. 'You *have* hurt yourself!'

He sounded outraged, Jill thought in vague wonderment. As though he really, really didn't want her to be injured. Or maybe he felt guilty. Did he think it was his fault because he hadn't insisted on doing the task himself? She opened her mouth to reassure him but couldn't say anything. The pain was overriding the ability to put any words together coherently.

'What's happened?' Jarred sounded frightened.

'Jill's hurt her finger.' Jack's voice was calm. In control. 'Can you go and find someone and ask if they've got some ice? There might be a fridge in the staffroom.'

'OK.' Jarred ran off, with Bella loping at his heels.

'Can you move it?' Jack asked.

'I don't think so. Not yet, anyway.'

'Can you feel me touching the end?'

'Yes.'

'Are these other fingers all right?'

'Yes.' Jill could feel his touch. Oddly, she trusted him not to hurt her any more, even when he touched the injured finger. She was quite happy to let him examine her—as though he knew what he was doing. Had he done a first-aid course of some kind or was it just a combination of common sense and caring?

Because he *did* care. She could feel it all the way into her bones. His touch. The tone of his voice.

The way he was looking at her.

'I hope it's not broken,' he said.

He was holding the eye contact and Jill couldn't look away.

'Even if it is, there's not much that can be done. I'll just have to strap it to the next door finger and keep it still for a while.'

'The ice should help, if Jarred can find some.'

'Yes.'

They were still staring at each other. He was still holding her hand.

They were so close. Only inches separated their faces. If Jill stood on tiptoe and tilted her face, she would be in the perfect position to be kissed.

She *wanted* to be kissed.

'I'll bet it hurts like hell,' Jack said.

'Yes.' But Jill wasn't thinking about the pain. She was busy drowning in Jack's eyes. Falling deeper.

Don't look at me like that.

The plea formed on Jack's lips but he couldn't utter the words.

A maelstrom of emotions were warring inside his head. In his heart.

The horror of seeing Jill hurt herself.

The fierce wish that he'd been able to protect her from harm. He *could* have. He should have.

The desire to make the pain go away. To make everything all right. And the frustration of knowing he couldn't.

The awakening of feelings he'd thought he couldn't have any more. Of caring too much.

Of letting people down.

If Jill kept looking at him like this, he would be unable to keep any distance at all and if he got any closer—even a hair's breadth—this woman was going to fall in love with him.

He could fall in love with her. Too easily.

And he would let her down because he wasn't capable of caring enough. He couldn't trust himself to commit to caring about anything because at some point it could become too much again. It would threaten to destroy him and he would have to stop caring. He would become a person like her ex-husband. A doctor just on the outside.

And that would destroy her.

'I can't do it,' he found himself murmuring aloud. 'I can' give you what you need, Jill.'

She didn't look away. Even as Jarred ran back toward

them with Miss Reynolds, who had a bowl of ice in her hands, and Faith, who was carrying a stack of teatowels.

'But I'm not asking for anything, Jack,' she said softly. 'Maybe I can give you something.' She even smiled. 'It's Christmas after all. We're allowed a little bit of magic.'

CHAPTER EIGHT

DR METCALF senior took one look at Jill's finger and groaned.

'This is a disaster!'

'It's not that bad, Dad. The colour and capillary refill are fine now and the sensation's almost back to normal. I don't think it's broken. Look, I can move it.' Jill managed to bend her finger a little. 'Ooh, ouch!'

'We should X-ray it.' Jim gave a resigned sigh. 'Have you seen how many people are in that waiting room?'

The noise had been impossible to ignore when they had trooped in minutes before. Muriel had been looking harassed as she'd filled in new patient forms and tried to establish order. Jack had taken one look and disappeared rapidly to tie Bella up in the garden and take Jarred upstairs to show off his ribbon to his siblings.

'Most of them are one family,' Jill said. 'Campers, I think, and it looks like the children all have a nasty dose of sunburn. A gallon of Calamine lotion and some paracetamol should do the trick. I can still deal with something like that.'

Jim was still staring gloomily at the offending finger. 'We'll strap it and give you some anti-inflammatories. If it's not any better later tonight we'll X-ray it. You can't be too careful with hands—especially when it's your dominant one.'

'I'm not planning on being a surgeon. Or a concert pianist. It can wait.' Jill held her breath as her father splinted her finger by strapping it to its neighbour with narrow sticky tape.

'It's not just the waiting room. Maisie called a few minutes ago. She's worried about one of your chickenpox kids. The youngest.'

'Nat?'

'Apparently he's spiked a fever and he's pretty miserable.'

'I'll go and have a look at him.'

'And then there's Betty. Angela says she didn't eat any lunch and seems very quiet. She's only a week post-op. She could be brewing an infection. Or a thrombus.'

'I'll check her out, too.'

'How are you going to manage? It'll be a bit difficult to look in that lad's ears or feel Betty's belly one-handed.'

'I'll manage. It feels much better now it's strapped.' Jill wiggled her hand experimentally. 'If I can't manage, or if I find something I'm worried about, I'll give you a call, OK?'

Jim just nodded. 'Send in that sunburnt family on your way out, would you?

Armed with her stethoscope, a tympanic thermometer and an otoscope, Jill made her way upstairs towards the wards.

Towards where Jack had gone.

Would he still be there? The tingle of anticipation at the possibility was too pleasurable to try toning it down despite a new misgiving.

She had seen that flash of fear in Jack's eyes back in the Ballochburn school's car park.

The need to offer reassurance had been overwhelming, which was why Jill had said she wasn't asking him for anything.

And she wasn't.

Yes, she realised she was falling in love with Jack Sinclair and she would desperately *like* him to kiss her.

Or more.

OK, a lot more.

But Jill knew this was just a blip in her life. An interlude that was going to last a few days at the most. A bit of Christmas magic.

Would it hurt to make the most of it?

Maybe Jack had been dropped into her life to let her know it was possible to feel this way again. Part of the reason she'd kept that wedding band on for so long had been as protection. To stop anyone trying to get close because she hadn't been anywhere near ready to try again.

She felt ready again.

Jack could be a little practice run. Training wheels before launching herself back into life properly.

At the top of the sweeping staircase, Jill paused for a moment, looking out the window to see if she could spot where Bella had been tied up. She was in the shade, which was good. Just beside that bench where Jack and Jarred had been sitting—had it only been yesterday?

Her breath escaped in a long sigh. She was kidding herself, wasn't she? The real truth was that she wanted a lot more than a set of training wheels. She couldn't have anticipated feeling this drawn to someone because, despite her ability to fall head over heels in love, she had never felt quite like *this* in her life.

Jack was amazing. Gorgeous. Kind. Mysterious.

She was suspicious, of course, that it couldn't come to anything, but what if caution stopped her even investigating? What if Jack left and she hadn't found out if the possibility of something was there? If she looked so hard she put herself off leaping even a tiny bit? It could be something she might regret for the rest of her life.

Jill turned away from the window. Jack probably wasn't even with the children any longer and she had work that needed to be done.

Her finger throbbed. Right up until she entered the disused four-bed ward that had been transformed into a nursery. A cot had been slotted in for Nat and the fourth bed was being used by Elise, who was keeping an eye on the children overnight. Hope was sleeping along the corridor in another empty ward.

The large girl was there now, joggling a red-faced, miserable toddler on her lap. Jade and Mel were sitting on another bed, discarded toys and games littering the floor around them. Jarred was teaching them a song.

Faith, Hope and Maisie were all watching with varying degrees of admiring smiles as the younger children chanted the words of the song Jarred must have picked up from his new friends in the school grounds.

'*We three kings of Orient are
One on a tractor, two in a car...*'

Jack was taking photos but he looked up as Jill entered and gave her a half-smile that made her heart trip and then speed up noticeably.

'*One on a scooter, tooting his hooter
Following yonder star...*'

Hope clapped her hands, beaming.

Faith nodded approvingly. 'A very famous man wrote that song. John Clark, his name was, except most people called him Fred Dagg.'

Jarred ducked his head. 'I can't remember the rest.'

'I can.' Jill grinned and then opened her mouth to sing. *'Oh, oh… Star of wonder, star of light. Star of bewdy, she'll be right…'*

Jack was chuckling now. A rich, joyous sound that widened Jill's smile further. Had he never heard the iconic Kiwi Christmas song?

'Star of glory, that's the story… Following yonder star…'

'Do it again,' Jade begged.

'Can't, sweetie. I've come to visit Nat, 'cos he's feeling sick.'

'He's getting the spots now,' Mel said.

'I thought he might be. How are *your* spots?'

'Itchy.'

'Getting scabby yet?'

'One of them is. Does that mean I can go out to play now?'

'Soon. When they're all scabby, like Jarred's.'

'Faith told me about that finger.' Hope was frowning sympathetically at Jill's hand. 'How's it feeling?'

'I'd actually forgotten about it,' Jill said in surprise. Amazing how a pleasant emotion could cancel out a negative one. She stole a glimpse at Jack, who was packing away his camera.

'It's only one more sleep till Christmas,' Jade said importantly. Then her face creased anxiously. 'Do you think Santa will know where we are?'

'Of course he will.' Hope exchanged a glance with Faith and Jill realized they had everything under control. These children would be getting some treats for Christmas. She disguised her pleased smile by directing it at Elise, who was holding Nat up towards her.

'No, you keep holding him, Elise. He seems happy enough for now.'

But Nat's face crumpled ominously as Jill approached so she looked over her shoulder at the older children. 'Hey, could you guys sing to Nat again? It might distract him while I take his temperature and try to look in his ears.'

To a much more confident rendition of their version of 'We Three Kings', Jill examined the toddler, who was entering the most miserable phase of this illness. Jill managed to listen to his chest and get enough of a glimpse into his ears and throat to be happy enough that he wasn't developing any sinister complications.

'We need to get his temperature down a bit and do something for this rash. I'll give him some paracetamol and then I think a bath with lots of lotion will be the best we can do for the moment. I'll come back and check him again after I've done a ward round.'

Jack chose to head off at the same time but when Jill went to veer into the geriatric and recuperative ward, he was spotted by the charge nurse, Angela.

'Just what I need,' she called. 'A *man*!'

'Ooh, your number's up,' Jill whispered.

'I hope not,' Jack whispered back. 'She must be sixty at least!'

'I can't reach the top of the tree,' Angela explained as she hurried to meet them. 'Even with the stepladder, I'm too short.' She peered over her half-moon spectacles at Jill. 'And you'd have to fly to get there.' With a warm smile she held out a large sparkly star to Jack. 'It'll only take a minute,' she said winningly.

Except that it took a lot longer, of course.

Who could fail to spot the photo opportunity of old arthritic hands busy attaching decorations to the lower limbs of the oversized pine tree? As far as these patients were concerned, being the potential pin-up models for a calendar was the most interesting thing that had happened for a long time.

Enid Hinkley was mumbling enthusiastically but nobody could understand a word.

'You need to put your teeth in,' Jill reminded her. She glanced over Enid's shoulder to where she could see Betty sitting in an armchair beside her bed, just watching the others.

She didn't see Enid pick up her walking stick but she heard the result as the elderly woman leaned forward to poke Jack.

'Oof!' he said. 'What was *that* for?'

'Enid!' Angela said disapprovingly. 'You know you're not supposed to poke people. It isn't polite.'

Enid mumbled more loudly.

'She wants to make sure you take *her* photo,' Angela translated for Jack, who was rubbing the back of his thigh.

Smothering a giggle, Jill went over to Betty—a woman in her seventies who had recently undergone a bowel resection and had come back to Ballochburn to recuperate.

'I hear you're not feeling so good, Betty?'

'Her temperature's up a bit.' Angela had followed Jill. 'Only 37.4, though.'

'How's the tummy feeling?'

'Not so bad,' Betty said. 'I'm all right. Just having an off day.'

'Let's get you up on the bed so I can have a proper look at you.'

It wasn't easy, examining a patient with the middle fingers of her right hand strapped together, and it was some minutes before Jill went to the phone on Angela's desk, near where the tree was being decorated. The silver and gold baubles were much thicker on the lower branches and tinsel was now being applied generously.

Jill dialled an internal extension number. 'You still busy, Dad?'

'Is the Pope Catholic?' She heard a faint sigh. 'I think I might have got rid of the last patient for now. Hope so, because Muriel reckons she's cooking up a migraine. I've just got a mountain of paperwork to do. How's the lad?'

'OK for now. A bit sad but I can't see anything worrying that's brewing. I'm hoping to get his temperature down, which should cheer him up.'

'And Betty?'

'Mild pyrexia. Heart rate's up a bit. Blood pressure's stable. She's got a bit of abdo tenderness, though, and the incision is definitely more inflamed than it was yesterday.'

'Infection?'

'Probably. I'll get a urine sample and we need bloods for a white-cell count and cultures, but I'll get her started on antibiotics stat.'

'Good. Sounds like you've got things sorted.'

'Yes. Um…'

Her father chuckled. 'You need me to take that blood sample, don't you?'

'Yes. Sorry, Dad. I know how busy you are. I'd ask Angela but she doesn't get much practice these days and Betty's veins aren't the best. And I certainly wouldn't be doing her any favours by trying it left-handed.'

Jack looked up from his position only a few feet from where Jill was standing. He opened his mouth as though about to say something but when Jill raised her eyebrows, he gave a subtle headshake and his gaze returned to the screen on his camera. Enid was in front of him, beaming toothlessly as she looped a long strand of tinsel over the end of a branch. What was that about? Jill wondered.

'I'm on my way,' Jim was saying. 'Have things set up, could you? Someone else could well arrive down here any minute.'

'Sure.'

It was no problem to collect the tourniquet, alcohol swabs, needle and test tubes. By the time Angela had filled in the labels, Jim had arrived on the ward. He looked out of breath.

'Are you OK, Dad?'

'I'm fine. I just ran up the stairs a bit fast, that's all.' Jim picked up the needle and smiled at Betty.

'This will hurt you more than it hurts me.'

'Get away with you.' Betty smiled. 'You wouldn't hurt a fly.'

'You haven't lost your touch, have you?' Jill commented seconds later. 'There's a lot of GPs out there who would have trouble with veins like Betty's.'

'It's one advantage of being run off your feet with a rural practice, I guess.' Jim handed the tubes to Angela. 'You don't get a chance to lose your touch. Let's put a plaster on this.'

He still seemed out of breath. Jill frowned. 'Are you sure you're feeling all right? You look pale.'

'Stop fussing, Jillian. You're as bad as your mother.' Jim smiled a farewell at Betty. 'I'll see you later when I come up to enjoy the carol singers.'

Heading for the door, Jim frowned at his daughter. 'Stop staring at me. I'm *fine*.'

But he didn't look fine at all. He looked a bit grey, was breathing too quickly, and had beads of perspiration on his forehead. Jill followed him, exchanging an anxious glance with Angela. The senior nurse gave her head a quick shake as though she agreed something wasn't right. Should Jill be more insistent or would that make things worse by getting her father's back up?

He was hardly likely to take any notice of her. Jill wished the last locum, Andrew, was still there. He'd have to listen to another doctor if it wasn't his child. She gave a 'What can I do?' kind of shrug and Angela looked as helpless as he felt.

Jim had reached the desk now. Jack had his black bag on the desk as he put his camera away. He was staring at the older doctor as Jim scribbled a note in Betty's file.

'What's wrong with your jaw?' Jack asked, after watching Jim scrubbing it with the knuckles of his free hand.

'A bit of toothache,' Jim growled. 'Don't *you* start!'

'Any chest pain?'

Jill had come to a halt beside her father. She stared at Jack. How on earth could he know that tooth pain could be an expression of cardiac problems?

'No,' Jim said.

'But you're short of breath.' Jack had a very intent, focussed look on his face. Jill felt invisible. 'Have you had anything like this happen before?'

'I just ran up the stairs too fast. I'll be fine. I'll sit down for a minute.'

Silently, Jill pulled out the chair from behind the desk and watched her father sink onto it. Jim's hand went into his shirt pocket as he sat down.

'Oh, my God!' Jill exclaimed. 'What's *that*?'

'GTN.' It was Jack who answered. 'You're having an angina attack, aren't you, Jim?'

'I know what it is,' Jill snapped. 'I just want to know why Dad's carrying it around with him.' She glared at Jack. 'How do you know what it is, anyway?'

But Jack's attention was completely on Jim. 'Have you seen a cardiologist?' he queried.

Jim shook his head. 'Don't need to.' He pulled the cap from the spray canister and raised it to his mouth.

'Hang on a tick.' Jack reached for his wrist. 'You don't want to be taking GTN if your blood pressure's low.' He nodded a second later. 'OK, your radial's fine—you can go ahead. Are you taking aspirin?'

'If I remember.' Jim scowled at Jack. 'You're a doctor, aren't you?'

'Not any more.' The headshake was decisive. 'But I can tell you what you need to do right now, and you might listen to me more than you would to your daughter.'

So he had stepped out of the closet because he'd seen her frustration at trying to get her father to admit something was wrong?

She wasn't about to appreciate his assistance, however. She was as stunned by the revelation as she was worried that her father might be having a heart attack. 'You don't just stop being a doctor. Or were you struck off?' Jill put her hand on her father's shoulder. 'I'm not sure you *should* be giving my dad any advice. I'll look after him.'

'I wasn't struck off,' Jack said quietly. 'Do you have a twelve-lead ECG machine available? Benchtop testing for cardiac enzymes, by any chance?'

Jim had taken two puffs of his spray under his tongue. He was leaning back in the chair with his eyes closed. 'It's easing off now,' he said.

'You still need an ECG. And bloods.' Jill managed to sound very firm. She could take over now.

'And don't forget the aspirin,' Jack added. 'Where's your ECG machine?'

'Downstairs. In the outpatient clinic.'

Jack looked at Angela. 'Do you have a wheelchair we could borrow?'

'You're not putting me in any damn wheelchair,' Jim muttered.

'We could put you into bed here, then,' Jack suggested calmly. 'And bring the machine up here.'

Jim glanced up to find Enid Hinkley grinning toothlessly at him. 'Oh, all *right*. I'll use the damn wheelchair.'

Jill had every intention of pushing the chair herself but couldn't help wincing as she put pressure on her injured hand. The chair started to turn in a circle.

'Let me push,' Jack offered.

'I can manage.' Jill gritted her teeth and straightened course. For some reason she didn't have time to try and analyse, Jack's revelation that he was a doctor and not a photographer wasn't stunning her any longer. It was making her angry.

Very, very angry.

'I can help,' Jack insisted.

'I can *manage*,' Jill snapped back.

'What about the ECG?' Jack queried politely. 'Can you attach all the leads one-handed? Can you take a blood sample from your father more easily than you could from Betty? Or get an accurate blood pressure even?'

Jill fumed in silence. She knew if she opened her mouth she would be as ungracious as her father in accepting assistance. She also knew, as well as he did, that assistance was necessary right now.

If Jim noted the grim silence in which he was trundled down to the clinic, he probably assumed it was because there was something to worry about. The tension only increased as they found people waiting there.

They stared at the trio, at the older man in the wheelchair, the young woman with a bandage on her hand and finally, with some relief, at Jack. 'Are you the doctor here?'

'I am,' Jill responded. 'I'll be with you as soon as I can.' She tried to smile reassuringly at Muriel, who was sitting behind her desk with her mouth open, staring in consternation at Jim. She could hardly tell her father's faithful receptionist not to worry, though, could she?

Not when she was worried sick herself.

It came as a huge relief to everybody that Jim's ECG showed no indication of a heart attack.

'There's not even any ST depression to speak of,' Jack noted. 'If you were having an angina attack, it seems to have resolved.'

Jim pulled his oxygen mask off. 'I don't need this, then. Didn't think so.' He sat up and swung his legs off the bed. 'The GTN is more than enough.'

'You need investigation,' Jack told him. 'A cardiac catheterisation, an echo and an exercise test would be a good idea, I think.'

'Maybe. If and when it gets any worse.'

'No Dad,' Jill said. 'You need to do it as soon as possible. I'll set it up.'

'Can't,' Jim said stubbornly. 'I'd have to take at least a whole day off. Probably two. I'll do it when I've got a new locum.'

'*I'm* your new locum,' Jill reminded him.

'Temporary.'

'Long enough. I'm here for weeks. There shouldn't be any problem setting up an appointment in that time.'

Jack nodded, as though the problem had been solved. 'What's your lipid profile like?' He smiled wryly at Jim's expression. 'You have no idea, do you? Doctors really do make the worst patients. What's your family history as far as cardiac disease goes?'

'How long has this been going on?' Jill interrupted. 'And why didn't you *say* something?'

'It's no big deal.' Jim sighed and took hold of Jill's uninjured hand, which he patted. 'I'm sorry, love. OK, I've had a bit of a niggle now and then and GTN fixes it so I've realised it's probably angina. But it seems to be stable. The same sorts of things bring it on, it's responsive to medication or rest and I'm not getting associated symptoms, so I'm sure I haven't had an infarct.'

'You were short of breath today.'

'I ran up the stairs.'

'You were grey and sweaty.'

'It's a hot day. I didn't get a chance to get one of those sausages at school and I forgot to get something later. I feel great now. No pain. No shortness of breath.'

Jill was unconvinced. 'You need to rest. I want you to lie in here and stay on that monitor.'

'No. There are patients waiting out there.'

Jack looked from father to daughter and back again. 'It might be a good idea,' he told Jim. 'At least for an hour or two. I've got the feeling your daughter is just about as stubborn as you are.'

Jim chuckled, the lines of tension finally leaving his face. 'She's worse, believe me.'

'I can help with any patients that turn up, if need be. My practising certificate is perfectly current. It's in my wallet, if you want to see it.'

'I'll trust you,' Jim said. 'You seem to know what you're talking about. And you're right—it's not worth the fight I'd have to have with Jill. I'll stay here and behave—but just until the carol singing. I wouldn't want to miss that.'

The thought of the choir reminded Jill of something else. 'Does Mum know you've been getting chest pain?'

'No. And you're not to say anything.'

Jill's lips folded into a mutinous line.

'She's been going on for years about the hours I work. This would give her the ammunition to try and force my retirement and you know I can't give it up.' There was a silent plea in her father's eyes that made Jill feel inexplicably sad. 'It's my life, Jilly. You—more than anyone—must understand that.'

'Let's get this blood sample. If we can get it to town, we should get a result by tonight. If it's normal, I won't say anything. Just yet.'

The same effort to hold her tongue was not going to apply to Jack Sinclair.

With the reassurance that her father wasn't in any imminent danger the anger Jill felt towards Jack resurfaced. And now she knew why she felt so angry.

Betrayed, even.

On an instinctive level, she had trusted this man. As much as her father trusted the fact he was a qualified doctor.

And Jack had not been honest with her.

She told him precisely that after they'd left her father under strict instructions to stay put and rest. In the short corridor that led to the waiting area, Jill paused, folded her arms and glared at Jack.

'You lied to me. You're not a photographer.'

'I am now.'

'It's not as if you didn't have the opportunity to tell me the truth. Good grief, you let me position your hands to show you how to stabilise that boy's neck as if you had no idea what you were doing. And up on the ward, you were thinking about offering to take Betty's blood sample, weren't you? When you heard me apologising for dragging Dad up there.'

'I made a decision to stop practising medicine. I need to stick to that.'

'So why didn't you "stick to that" when it was obvious Dad was having an angina attack?'

'I could see he wasn't going to listen to you. That you needed help.'

Jill wasn't going to let the fact that Jack had been trying to help her count for anything. 'You just couldn't help yourself, that's the real reason. You don't just stop being a doctor.' She gave an incredulous huff. 'There I was, blathering on about how it's more to do with who you are than what you do for a living. You knew exactly what I was talking about, didn't you?'

Or had he? He hadn't been interested in hearing Emma's story. Jill could recall the disappointment that he hadn't seemed to care. Her tone became scathing.

'I suppose you were one of those medics who do see it as just a job. The ones who can stay as uninvolved as possible.'

He flinched visibly. He even had the nerve to look outraged. *'No!'*

'So you just got bored, then?' It was easy to direct the

anger at allowing herself to fall in love with another wrong person—another person who wasn't trustworthy—towards Jack. To make this *his* fault. She could get over this nice and quickly. She could just dump her disappointment and frustration and even her worry about her father's situation right where it belonged.

On top of Jack Sinclair.

'What sort of doctor *were* you, Jack? A dermatologist? Pathologist? Psychiatrist?'

'An emergency physician, if you really want to know.'

'No, I don't think I do.' Jill turned away with a dismissive flick of her curls. 'I doubt that I'd believe what you said, and what does it matter anyway? You'll be gone in a day or two.'

Jack's voice behind her was quiet. Controlled. 'Would you rather I left now?'

Jill had to turn back. 'So you'd be happy to take off and let people down? How's Jarred going to feel when he thinks you're here for Christmas Day? What about Aunty Faith? You agreed to take the photographs for that calendar she's so excited about.' Jill dragged in a ragged breath. 'Not that I'm surprised. If you can just give up medicine, I don't suppose it matters to you if you let people down.' This time she wasn't going to turn back. She gave Jack one last, supremely disappointed look. 'You just don't give a damn, do you? If you want to go, that's fine by me.'

CHAPTER NINE

IT WAS hardly surprising that Ballochburn's interdenominational church choir had traditional red robes and frilly white collars. Or that they held matching candlesticks that glinted from fresh polishing.

With Faith as their conductor, things were being done properly.

Jill's mother was in the middle of a semi-circle arranged according to height. To one side, Judith Cartwright sat bolt upright in front of a small portable electronic keyboard. The choir sang perfectly in tune and there was no nonsense about pukekos in ponga trees or wise men on scooters. The old favourites of 'Silent Night', 'Away in a Manger' and 'Hark the Herald Angels Sing' filled the ward.

Jarred sat on the floor beside Enid Hinkley's armchair, staring in fascination at the movement of Wally Briggs's moustache as he added a gloriously rich baritone to the range of feminine voices.

Jack stood to one side, camera in hand, staring in equal fascination at the play of candlelight on Jill Metcalf's golden curls. She was still deliberately avoiding his gaze. Still furious with him, no doubt.

The image of the Christmas angel she had represented had receded rather sharply since the verbal attack he had been subjected to. This woman was quite capable of being stubborn and intolerant. Why had he thought she would understand if he'd spilled his guts, as he'd been tempted to do when they had been sitting beside the river? Just as well confusion had helped him hold his tongue. He'd been wrong to think that Jill had all the answers.

This was *his* problem.

Something he had to work through in his own time and in his own way.

Why did it matter so much that Jill's opinion of him was now so low?

Why had he stayed to continue his obligation to take these damned calendar photographs?

The knot in his gut was anger, that's why. A familiar resentment that he'd somehow been dropped on the wrong side of the bed at birth or something. The confirmation that nobody would ever bother getting to know who he really was.

Or care enough about that person.

What was really holding him back was that there was someone else who was in danger of feeling the same way. A nine-year-old boy who was coming out of his shell thanks to the illusion of the parallel universe.

Jack wasn't going to be the one to bring reality crashing in around Jarred. Not today, on the eve of Christmas. Not in the midst of the magic of candlelight and music and the brightly wrapped parcels that had mysteriously appeared under the twinkling tree.

He had been wrong to think that he had nothing to give

anyone. He could talk to Jarred. Tell him he was a terrific kid and how important he was going to be to his brothers and sister in the years to come. That things would get better in time. Give him something to hang onto during the tough times that were sure to come.

Because things would get better. For himself as well. Maybe this was all an illusion but it had shown him he was capable of feeling again. He cared about Jarred. Given a chance, he could have cared about Jill.

Too much.

It wasn't meant to be but it had demonstrated that it could be possible. With someone. Some time.

He had been given the kind of hope he'd like to give Jarred. And he knew just how valuable a gift that could be.

The carol service finished at 9 p.m. Quite late for the three young children who had been given the treat of gathering in the corridor, well away from the ward, to listen to the carols.

Nat had fallen asleep on Elise's shoulder, which was a good sign he wasn't feeling too miserable any more. His colour was also looking better, Jill noted with satisfaction.

Maisie detached herself from the small group as she saw Jill coming out of the ward, with the choir and other spectators trailing behind her.

'You get these kiddies to bed,' she directed Elise. 'I'll bring you up some hot chocolate when the choir's had their supper.'

Jarred hung back, shifting from foot to foot, waiting for Jill to finish the call she had just answered on her mobile phone.

'Can I go and say good night to Bella? Please?'

'I'm sorry, hon.' Jill had to refuse the request. 'I have to go out on a call.'

'What's happened?' Jim turned from the conversation he was having with Wally Briggs.

'It's Sue,' Jill said simply. 'She's asking for me.'

'Oh…' The sound of comprehension hung in the air and conversation around them trickled into silence.

'I'd better come, too,' Jim said heavily.

'Poor wee mite,' someone said sadly, 'I was really hoping she'd last until Christmas Day.'

Jill had to swallow hard. She put her hand on her father's arm and gave it a squeeze. 'There's no need.'

There was no need to say anything else. People with sombre faces made way for Jill. She could hear Jarred behind her, sounding bewildered but brave.

'I could go by myself. I know where the shed is.'

'It's OK, mate.' Jack's voice. 'I'll come with you. I could do with some fresh air.'

Long after Jarred had gone to bed, after the walk with Bella and the long talk they'd had, Jack was still up. Sitting in the dark, quiet garden. A glance at his watch showed him it was after midnight.

Christmas Day and here he was, in the last place he could have expected to be—a hospital.

Feeling things he had never expected to feel.

Concern for Jarred. Empathy. Satisfaction, almost, that he *could* feel that empathy and offer hope for a future. And, curiously, an extraordinary release in having told someone else about his own childhood.

He'd been sitting here for nearly two hours, just experiencing these emotions.

Feeling alive again.

Not that everything he was feeling was positive. Far from it. Jack had had to remember things he'd vowed to put behind him for ever. To share them with a nine-year-old boy who'd left, looking at him as though he was some kind of hero.

So different from the way Jill had last looked at him. As though he had disappointed her too much for it to be tolerable. The way her ex-husband had disappointed her?

That hurt.

It hurt so much he could add it to that background anger of feeling misunderstood because nobody—especially Jill Metcalf—cared enough to try and find out who he really was.

But it was his own fault, wasn't it?

How could anyone know who he was when he had locked it away so completely?

He'd never tried to find out if someone could care about him because he'd never revealed who he was—to anyone. He'd been hiding his whole life.

Fearing rejection.

Sabotaging any relationships he'd ever tried. Preventing anyone from getting too close. Protecting himself.

Right now, the person who knew him the best was sleeping in a room with his younger siblings. Probably dreaming about a life that included a scruffy dog he'd fallen in love with.

Jarred hadn't rejected him. He'd been stunned to hear about Jack's history. Disbelieving at first and then…overawed. The way the boy had gathered his own courage and strengthened himself to face the future had actually been visible in the way those skinny shoulders had straightened. In the very adult eye contact that had expressed both amazement and gratitude.

Love, even.

Jack had promised he'd stay in touch. He was going to give

Jarred his mobile phone as a Christmas gift. He would get himself a replacement and then they could stay in contact. He would keep Jarred's phone topped up and they could communicate by text messaging or calls. For as long as Jarred needed a mentor. A parent figure if he wanted one. One that wasn't going to disappear from his life.

The thought of what the gift would symbolise gave Jack the best feeling. A glow that stayed with him as he made his way through the darkened corridors of the old hospital. Up the sweeping staircase and past the wards to get to the apartment over the kitchens.

The large, shadowy shape lurking upstairs gave him a fright.

'What the *hell*?'

They were too trusting in this neck of the woods. Doors weren't locked. No security. A middle-aged nurse on duty in the geriatric ward and a teenager watching over a roomful of children. One pint-sized female doctor who was currently miles away and another doctor who was at least minutes away in his own house and was way past running to protect anyone from a low-life who might be on the search for drugs.

But it wasn't a low-life. It was the teenager, Elise, and in the faint glow of moonlight Jack could see she looked far from happy.

'What's wrong, Elise?'

'I've got a sore tummy. I think it must have been those mince pies I had for supper. I've just been to the toilet.'

'Did that help?'

'No.'

Jack took hold of the girl's wrist. Her pulse was racing 'Where does it hurt, exactly?'

'All over.'

'Is it there all the time or does it come and go?'

'It's there all the time but it gets worse and then a bit better. Kind of in waves.'

'Can you describe the pain? Is it sharp? Dull? Did it come on suddenly?'

'It's just been getting worse and worse. It's like a really bad cramp.'

'Like period pain?'

'Yes. Only worse.'

'Have you had anything like this before?'

'No.'

'Are you feeling unwell in any other way? Hot and cold, maybe? Have you been vomiting?'

'No. It's just my tummy.'

Her skin felt damp and Jack could hear the faint gasp of over-rapid breathing. Whatever this pain was caused by, it had to be significant. Appendicitis? Ovarian cyst or torsion?

'I'm going to take you downstairs,' he told Elise. 'I need to see what's going on. Have a look at your tummy and take your blood pressure and things.'

'But—'

'It's OK. I'm a doctor.'

'But I can't leave the children. I felt bad enough, going to the toilet.'

'I'll wake Hope up and tell her what's happening.'

He was back within a couple of minutes. 'All sorted. Do you think you'll be able to walk?'

Elise nodded. 'It's not so bad again now.'

But she had to stop halfway down the stairs. To sit down, doubled over, groaning with the pain. By the time Jack got her as far as the surgery and flicked on some lights, he was really worried.

He should call Jim. Hand over the responsibility of this unexpected patient.

Except he couldn't. Jim was, hopefully, sound asleep. Resting. The last thing he needed was the stress of an emergency that could bring on another angina attack. Or worse, given that they couldn't know how serious his heart condition was.

He should ring Jill on her mobile but he couldn't do that either. Not when she was with her best friend who had just lost her small child.

Elise was reluctant to climb onto the narrow bed. 'It hurts.'

'I know.' Jack put his arm around the girl to assist her. His hand was in contact with her belly. It felt rigid.

Peritonitis? An appendix that had already burst? But she hadn't seemed unwell. Hadn't been running a temperature or complaining of any abdominal pain. She had seemed fine when she'd been holding Nat as Jill had examined the toddler earlier.

And her stomach didn't feel rigid by the time she was lying flat on the bed.

It felt…odd.

'Elise?' Jack took a deep, steadying breath. 'Is there any chance that you're pregnant?'

The silence was unnerving. So was the way Elise refused to meet his gaze.

'How far along are you?'

'I don't know.' Elise burst into tears. 'My boyfriend dumped me when he finally found out, just like I knew he would. And my mum threw me out.'

Was she anywhere near full term? Jack felt her abdomen

more thoroughly. Elise wasn't small by any means. She could easily have concealed a pregnancy for months. He could feel the shape of the baby beneath a thick layer of flesh. It seemed to be well down. Engaged. And then the muscles beneath his hands contracted again.

Elise groaned and the sheet beneath her bunched as she grabbed fistfuls of the white cotton.

'I've got to get these track pants off you,' Jack said tersely. 'And see what's happening. You're in labour, Elise.'

'Oh… *No-o-o!*'

Jack had to agree. This was hardly appropriate—undressing a teenage girl in a deserted clinic.

And if she was giving birth to a premature baby, there were far too many things that could go wrong. And they were far too far away from any back-up.

Jack did not want to be doing this. He could feel beads of perspiration breaking out, along with the grim realisation that he had no choice.

But then he forgot about himself. The sight of a crowning infant's head drove any personal baggage into oblivion. He could only hope that nothing would go wrong. Check that the umbilical cord wasn't around the baby's neck. Support the tiny body as it emerged and keep it head down to prevent fluid getting into its lungs.

Astonishingly, it seemed to be a good size. It opened its mouth and took a first breath. Let it out in a warbling cry.

'It's a girl,' Jack said.

'Oh…' Elise struggled to prop herself up on her elbows. She saw her baby and burst into tears again. 'Oh, my God!'

'She's absolutely fine.' Jack was watching the baby pink up and move its limbs. He could feel a strong, rapid heartbeat.

The crying had stopped by the time he clamped and cut the cord but the baby still looked fine. It seemed to be watching him with eyes so dark they looked black. Watching and…trusting.

He helped Elise sit up against the pillows and placed the infant in her arms. 'I need to find some towels,' he said. He frowned as he saw how Elise was shivering violently in the aftermath of giving birth. 'And some blankets.'

He opened cupboard doors but couldn't find what he needed. 'I'll be back in a tick,' he said.

He opened the door to the surgery and almost walked straight into the figure of Jill Metcalf.

She looked pale and drawn. And also very worried. 'I saw the lights on,' she said sharply. 'What's going on?'

The baby gave another cry behind him and Jill's jaw dropped.

'Elise,' Jack said succinctly. 'She's just given birth. Can you show me where you keep your towels?'

'I just don't believe it.'

'It was a surprise, that's for sure.'

Jill stopped walking. Despite the fact it was 2 a.m. and she had agreed to go home and sleep, she was reluctant to leave the hospital grounds. Maybe that reluctance had been why she hadn't refused Jack's offer to accompany her through the gardens.

They had only got as far as the big tree with the bench underneath it. The one Jill would always think of as being Jack and Jarred's bench from now on. Without thinking, she sat down.

'Life's so weird sometimes, isn't it? I come from a family who's just lost their precious daughter and find a new life in the world. Another little girl.'

'Life does go on, I guess, even if we don't feel ready for it.' Jack sat down beside her. 'Was it terrible at the Wheelers'?'

'Yes and no. The grief is dreadful, of course, but the strength of that family is amazing. The love they have for each other will get them through this. I didn't need to stay. I…couldn't…'

Jack simply nodded. 'Sometimes it's too hard, isn't it?'

Jill sat silently for a moment. She could feel the comfort from Jack's presence—the way she had when she had first told him about Emma—and it drove away any residual anger from the way he'd lied to her.

Jack understood. He had to know exactly how hard this was. She shouldn't have said those things about him just being a doctor on the outside. It wasn't true. It didn't matter what he chose to do for a living for the rest of his life, he could only understand because he was capable of feeling this way himself.

Of caring. *Really* caring.

'Why did you give up medicine, Jack?'

'I lost the capacity to care about what I was doing.'

'I don't believe that. I saw the way you looked tonight when you were holding Elise's baby. And the way you couldn't help yourself taking care of my dad yesterday afternoon. You're a born doctor, Jack.' She touched his hand. 'You care a lot.'

He moved his hand away from her touch. 'It's easy enough to care when things don't go wrong.'

Jill thought about that for a minute, aware of the peaceful warmth of a summer's night enveloping them. Of the intimacy of sitting together like this, with only the croak of frogs and the rustle of a nearby hedgehog to break the silence.

Until she spoke very softly. 'What went so wrong for you?'

Jack sighed. 'Lots of things. Too many bad cases. Seeing things that shouldn't have happened. Feeling responsible.'

'Like?'

'Like the guy who had chronic back pain and had made it worse by trying to dig a tree stump out of his lawn. Seemed like an uncomplicated case. I took his history, gave him pain relief and organised X-rays and a scan.'

'Exactly what I would have done.' Jill nodded.

'And how would you have felt when he died an hour later from an undiagnosed triple A?'

Jill swallowed. 'Terrible—of course. But it happens, Jack. Especially with something like an aortic aneurysm that can rupture catastrophically. Even if you'd known exactly what it was, he might well have not made it.'

'I know. And if a GP hadn't sent one little kid home with his sore ears it might still have been too late but it was me who got him in ED a few hours later. Comatose from meningitis. He died before we could get him anywhere near Intensive Care.'

'You can't take responsibility for cases like that. It would break anyone.'

'I know that, too. I learned to step back from getting too involved. I had a great role model in my senior consultant. He was one of those doctors you mentioned—the ones who don't give a damn. The ones who see medicine as just a job.'

Like she'd accused Jack of being. How wrong had she been?

'I thought that was the way forward. The way everybody copes.'

'No,' Jill said quietly. 'Not people like my dad.'

'Or you.'

'I don't think it worked for you either, did it, Jack?'

He snorted. 'No.'

'So what happened? What was the last straw that made you give it all up?'

'A five-year-old boy who got clipped by a truck when he ran out onto a pedestrian crossing. Multi-trauma. His mother was so hysterical we had to send her out of Resus.'

Jack leaned forward, his forehead resting on his hand as he continued speaking. Slowly at first. Quietly. As though talking to himself. Jill had to resist the urge to touch him again. To take hold of his hand. She didn't want to break what felt like a spell of connection. A mystery unfolding.

'I had him on oxygen. Fifteen litres a minute but his sats were only eighty-nine percent. I listened to his chest and there was no sign of a pneumothorax. I bag-masked him and got the sats up to ninety-eight percent, no problem. He needed intubation to protect his airway and give him adequate oxygenation.'

Jill just listened. Jack cleared his throat and spoke more rapidly, as though remembering the urgency of the situation.

'I couldn't visualise the vocal cords. Sucked out a heap of blood and tried again but there was obviously trauma. The sats were dropping again so I bag-masked and called for back-up. My consultant arrived. He asked me if there was a pneumothorax and when I said no, he told me to try again with intubation. I said I was worried about the possibility of laryngeal trauma and oedema and queried calling Anaesthesia for an emergency tracheotomy. He said we didn't want to chop a hole in the kid's neck unless it was absolutely necessary.'

Jill could sense the impending disaster. She found she was holding her breath.

'I'll cut a long story short,' Jack said bitterly. 'The attempt at intubation failed again. The kid's condition deteriorated. Finally, my consultant gave a bored kind of shrug, reached for some gloves and ordered someone to get him a tracheotomy kit.'

He took a long, slow breath. 'It was too late. I had known it would be too late. I watched the nurse swab that little neck and the consultant take his time identifying the landmarks. The child had been without oxygen for too long by then. Even if he survived he'd be brain damaged. And it took way too long to do the procedure. There was a lot of damage and too much bleeding. The boy went into cardiac arrest well before the tube got placed. I was doing compressions. I knew it was futile but I had to try and do *something*.'

'That's horrible,' Jill murmured.

Jack glanced up. 'You know what the worst thing was?'

'What?'

'There I was, doing the compressions, and I look down and this kid had a plaster on his knee. One of those cartoon character ones with someone like Goofy or Donald Duck on it. It really hit me that someone loved this boy. Looked after him. I thought of all the grazed knees I'd had that had never got a plaster put on them.'

A wave of shock hit Jill.

This wasn't just about a man who had been unable to cope with the emotional pressure of being a doctor.

It was about someone who was thirty-three years old and had never been properly loved.

She hadn't imagined that haunted look the first time she had seen his face. It hadn't just been a flight of fancy when his eyes had reminded her of those belonging to a lost and frightened dog hiding behind rubbish bins.

This wasn't the familiar squeeze of compassion Jill could feel gripping her heart at this moment. It was more like a cramp. Painful and raw.

'We worked on that kid for forty minutes.' Jack had returned to speaking quietly. To himself. 'And finally my consultant stripped off his gloves, threw them in the bin and called the time of death. Then he turned to me and said, "Go and tell the mother."'

'Oh, *God*,' Jill whispered in horror.

'I did it,' he said flatly. 'I even held it together. Gave the poor woman the usual spiel about how we'd done everything possible and how sorry we were, but it wasn't true and I didn't feel that I had. I couldn't feel anything at all. It was like I'd died inside when I'd noticed that plaster. I knew then that I had to get out and it's been that way ever since.'

'You're not dead inside, Jack. Not by a long shot.'

'Maybe not. I've certainly been feeling things again since I arrived here. There's something about this place.' Jack looked up properly for the first time since he'd started talking about himself. He caught Jill's gaze and held it. Picked up her hand and held that as well.

'Something about you, I think,' he added with a gentle smile. 'I suspect it's magic. You and this place together.'

Jill squeezed his hand. 'It's not really magic. It's just that this place is my rock. You've never had a rock, have you, Jack?'

He shook his head. 'I guess that's what I need to find.'

I could be your rock, Jill wanted to say. I could love you and nurture you and give you the strength you need to be who you really are.

Because she knew that was a person it was more than well worth being.

The words remained unuttered, however. A rock that was forced into your hand could just become a dead weight, couldn't it? It was something you had to choose for yourself. Something you recognised the value of enough to want to keep it with you for ever. They had only just met each other. It seemed crazy that she could feel so sure. She certainly couldn't blame Jack if he had no inkling of a similar feeling.

Instead, she nodded agreement. 'A rock is an emotional bank. You can take what you need out but you have to have an open account and you have to put funds back whenever you can. You're just bankrupt at the moment, Jack, that's all. You've given too much and nobody's given enough back to you.'

She wanted to cry. It was easy enough to adopt a stray dog and give it love and find it a home. Her mother had proved how you could help the kind of children Jack must have been, at least temporarily. But did she have the right to offer anything to Jack? When she wasn't even going to be in the country for much longer?

'You'll find it, Jack. It might be a place—like this one.'

'There aren't any other places like this.'

'It could be a person. Someone you'll fall in love with who feels the same way about you.'

Would he say something? Even a hint that he might see her as a contender for that person?

She didn't have to leave. It didn't take a huge stretch of her well-polished imagination to think of staying here.

With Jack.

Taking over from her father—as a team.

Why would she need to leave the place her heart belonged if everything she could want was right here?

A career as a doctor.

A man she could love with her whole heart.

A family of their own somewhere down the track.

Jack had a lump the size of Africa in his throat. He couldn't swallow. Couldn't speak.

He knew exactly what he needed as his rock.

Jill.

But she deserved so much better than damaged goods. Why would she look at someone like him who couldn't guarantee he could cope with commitment? Why would she trust him when he couldn't trust himself?

Maybe, one day, when he had sorted himself out properly, he could risk rejection and offer her his heart.

But not now. Not when he was in the painful process of a kind of rebirth. It would take time to deal with all this emotional stuff again and not feel so vulnerable.

'It's time I went,' he said finally. He withdrew his hand from Jill's and stood up.

'What?' Jill gazed up at him in dismay. 'You're going to leave Ballochburn? *Now?*'

Jack grinned. 'Actually, I just meant it's time I went to bed.' Then his smile faded. 'But it is time I left Ballochburn. If I don't start looking, I'm never going to find my rock, am I?'

'Not today,' Jill said with an audible gulp. 'Not on Christmas Day.'

'No. I can't leave on Christmas Day. I have a present I want to give someone. Jarred. I'm going to give him my phone so we can stay in touch.'

'Oh-h-h…' Jill got to her feet. She was smiling as she stood on tiptoe. 'That's so nice.'

And then her arms were around his neck and she seemed to get taller. Or was Jack leaning down? Whatever. She kissed him. Or he kissed her. Just a gentle brush of their lips.

They pulled apart instantly. Just far enough to look at each other. Jill's eyes were wide and shining. Her lips were parted. The invitation was, quite simply, totally irresistible.

Jack lowered his head and kissed her.

Properly.

CHAPTER TEN

'SHE had *what*?'

'A baby, Maisie. A dear little baby.'

'Who had a baby?' Jim must have been drawn to the smell of bacon filling Ballochburn Hospital's kitchens.

'Elise. Last night, just after midnight.' Jill threw her arms around her father. 'Merry Christmas, Dad!'

'I'm not sure what's merry about it so far,' Maisie grumbled. 'That lass didn't even tell me she was expecting.'

'You're miffed because you didn't spot it for yourself,' Jill teased. She went to steal a piece of bacon from the large cast-iron pan but got her fingers smacked.

'You can just wait your patience, Jilly Metcalf. I've had that girl lifting piles of linen and scrubbing floors, *that's* what I'm "miffed" about.'

'Didn't do her any harm. She's fine,' Jill reported happily. 'And so's the baby. All seven healthy pounds of her.'

'Who delivered it?'

'I did.' Jack walked into the kitchen in time to hear Jim's question. 'Nice, straightforward delivery, if somewhat unexpected. No complications.'

Maisie was appalled. 'What do you think you're doing, Jack Sinclair? Going round delivering people's babies?'

'Jack's a doctor,' Jim told her. 'A very good one, I suspect.'

'No!' Maisie looked more than miffed now. She looked hurt at the apparent size of the loop she'd been excluded from.

'I got there just a few minutes later,' Jill added soothingly. 'And none of us knew Jack was a doctor until yesterday.'

'Why not?' Maisie asked.

Good question, Jill thought. Not that she was about to answer it. She couldn't quite meet Jack's gaze either. For a moment all rational thought deserted her and all she could think of was that kiss they had shared last night. Or rather in the early hours of Christmas morning.

A kiss like no other Jill had ever experienced. One that she might not be lucky enough to ever experience again.

Hungry. Gentle. Passionate. Asking questions she had been only too happy to answer. Except she hadn't given the right answers, had she? Why else would Jack have walked away? Come back to place one more tender kiss on her lips? Then he had really gone, with a smile but without saying a single word of farewell.

'Why didn't someone call me?' Jim demanded.

'You needed to rest,' Jack reminded him. 'How are you feeling this morning, anyway?'

Maybe there hadn't been anything more Jack could have said after that kiss. He'd already said so much. Did he regret revealing as much as he had? Letting her in somewhere that Jill suspected no one else had ever been invited?

'I'll feel a whole lot better when I've had some breakfast,' Jim muttered.

'You'll have to eat fast,' Maisie warned. 'There's a heap to do round this place if Christmas dinner's going to make it to the table.'

Jim was still muttering as he sat down at the table. 'It's not right, waking up to an empty house on Christmas morning. First time it's happened in thirty-five years.'

'Sorry, Dad, but you weren't up and I *had* to nip over and see how Elise and the baby were doing.'

'She's doing just fine.' Hope came into the kitchen, holding a bundle of fluffy towelling. She peered down at the tiny face in the middle of the bundle. 'Aren't you, darling?' Hope glanced up at her husband. 'Merry Christmas, Jim.'

'Merry Christmas,' he returned gruffly.

The greeting was strained, but it would be, wouldn't it? They were the first words this couple had spoken directly to each other in days.

Jack had his camera out to catch the tiny starfish hand that had escaped the swaddling and seemed to reach out to the appreciative audience.

'Has she got a name yet?'

'No. Elise says she's a Christmas baby so she needs a special name.'

Jill looked at her father. He was the one who always had the original ideas when it came to names. But Jim was more interested in the plates of bacon and eggs and mushrooms that Maisie was delivering to the table.

'Eat up,' she ordered, 'while I get the trays up to the wards. And I've got a job for everybody after that.'

'But, Maisie, I've got a Christmas present for you,' Jill said.

'It'll have to wait,' Maisie said firmly. 'It's almost 7:00 a.m. and I'm not delivering a cold breakfast on Christmas Day. Faith would have my guts for garters if there were any complaints.'

* * *

Right on cue, Faith arrived.

'I hope those children didn't wake up too early,' she said. 'Come on, Jillian. It's time for Christmas.'

'Coming.' Jill stuffed a last crunchy piece of bacon into her mouth. She was still chewing it as she picked up the bag of gifts Faith and Hope had hurriedly put together yesterday. The toys and games weren't new but it would hardly matter to a bunch of children who had nothing, would it?

Jack followed, camera still in hand. 'Wouldn't be Christmas without the kids,' he said to no one in particular, 'and this is going to be a Christmas calendar, isn't it?' He had that small package for Jarred ready, Jill noticed—using up space in his camera bag.

Hope was already back in the children's room, helping Elise as she fed the infant. Nat was bouncing up and down in his cot in the corner and Jarred was still asleep. Jade and Mel were sitting up in bed, rubbing sleep from their eyes, staring at the small Christmas tree in the corner of their room. A tree that looked just as empty underneath as it had when they'd gone to sleep last night.

Faith poked her head around the door. 'Are you ready, children?'

Silent, wary nods. Jarred woke up, swung himself out of bed to rush to the tree and then stopped abruptly, an expression of resigned disappointment on his face.

'Told you he wasn't real,' he said to Mel and Jade.

Mel looked shocked. Jade's eyes filled with tears.

'Who said I wasn't real?' boomed a masculine voice. The tall figure, in full red regalia, black boots and an oddly rectangular shape to his huge belly, stood framed in the doorway. The walrus moustache didn't quite match the snowy white beard but who was going to notice? Jill could just make out Jack in the background, camera poised.

'Ho, ho, ho!' said Santa.

The children shrieked gleefully. Jarred couldn't quite manage the nonchalant air he was striving for. He managed half of it, with a suspicious scowl and his hands in his pockets, but then he saw the sack bulging with gifts and his eyes widened as he grinned.

'Awesome,' he said.

'Sorry I'm a bit late,' Santa boomed. 'Ballochburn is a bit out of the way, you know.'

Jim Metcalf slipped into the room as the children excitedly tore into parcels. The Friends of the Hospital had done themselves proud and there were plenty of new gifts of toys and clothing for the family. Nat was more interested in the wrapping paper than the contents of the gifts, apart from the floppy pink rabbit that had been one of Jill's childhood favourites. Already soft and worn with one eye missing, the toddler pressed it against his cheek as though greeting a long-lost friend.

It was Nat that Jim headed for.

'Thought I'd better pop up and see how the young fella was doing,' he said offhandedly to Jill.

'He's a lot better.' Jill scooped up both Nat and the pink rabbit for a cuddle. 'Still running a fever but paracetamol is wonderful stuff.'

Jim's grunt was satisfied but he didn't leave the room. He watched, along with the other adults present, as Jade tried on a pair of angel wings and fitted the headband with the tinsel halo over her wispy blonde hair.

'I'm the Christmas angel,' she announced. 'Jack! Jack! Take my photo!'

But Jack was busy, crouched beside Jarred, explaining the workings of the mobile phone to him.

'It's OK,' Jarred said. 'I know how to use a phone. Everybody does.'

'Cool. As soon as I get my new phone, I'll text you the number.'

Jarred just nodded. A casual observer might have thought he was less than impressed with the gift, but Jill saw the shy look he gave Jack a moment later.

The smile that passed between man and boy suggested a bond no one else would ever share.

A bit like the smile Jack had given her, just before he'd finally turned and walked away after that kiss.

She wished she had a gift for Jack.

She did—a huge gift—but would he want to accept it?

Her instincts had not been wrong this time. Jack was a lot more, rather than less, special than the man she had fallen in love with. His problem wasn't that he didn't care. He did. Too much.

Would he want to care about her? Would he consider accepting the gift she was prepared to give?

Her heart and soul. To have and to hold. From this day forward…

Probably not, Jill decided, which was why he'd walked away in silence last night. He wasn't ready for such a gift. He had things he needed to sort out for himself first. Having to blink the threat of tears from her eyes, she found it helpful to focus on her father as he moved further around the room.

To where Elise sat in an armchair, feeding a baby that was now sucking like an expert.

'Everything OK?' he queried casually.

'I guess. I'm sorry I didn't tell you I was pregnant when

you gave me the job, Dr Metcalf. I didn't think this would happen while I was here.'

'Just as well it did. I don't care what they say these days, a hospital is still the best place to have a baby.'

Elise looked down at her infant. 'She's beautiful, isn't she?' She looked up at Jim. 'I can't believe she's mine, you know? Someone I can love who will love me back.'

Jim cleared his throat and Jill could see the way he blinked. Exactly the same way she had a moment ago, when she had been thinking about Jack. Go, Elise, she applauded silently. Hit him in that soft spot and you'll have a job for life here if you want it.

Elise seemed to catch her thoughts. 'I know it won't be easy,' she said, 'but I reckon I can make it work. I've got a job already…that is, if you'll let me keep it for a while.'

'I'll see what we can do.' Jim was silent for a moment. 'I hear you're thinking of a Christmas name for this wee dot.' The casual tone didn't fool Jill. Acceptance was definitely on the agenda here. Love for her father made her eyes decidedly misty. A glance at her mother showed that Hope was also listening to the exchange. She looked misty-eyed, too.

'Mary's a bit boring,' Elise said. 'And I don't like Ivy. Or Joy, particularly. Angel's too cheesy. Holly's nice but lots of people call their babies Holly these days.'

'What about Carol?' Jim suggested.

'Like a Christmas carol? I hadn't thought of that.' Elise looked down at her baby again. She bent to brush a soft kiss on the downy head. 'I like it,' she said. 'A carol's a kind of song and songs are always happy.'

Jim smiled. He sighed with satisfaction. 'I'd best get going,' he said. 'I need to make sure Santa hasn't found a supply of medicinal sherry or something. We'll see you later, at lunchtime.'

He didn't seem to notice the way Hope stared after him as he left, blinking away tears of her own.

Jill was tempted to rush after her father. To drag him back and insist that he sort out the silly disagreement with Hope, which had grown out of all proportion. How could they let it continue? On Christmas Day?

It was only the stern look from Faith that prevented Jill following her impulse. Yes. Her parents did need to figure out what was important all by themselves or it might not be meaningful enough.

Just like Jack needed to do.

Her heart sank more than a fraction. It was going to be a bitter-sweet Christmas by the look of things. Tears and laughter. Joy and sorrow.

She would just have to try and make the most of the joyful bits.

A call out to the camping grounds just after Maisie had presented Jill with a bucket of fresh peas to shell seemed anything but a nuisance. Jill positively beamed at Jack.

'Hooray! I was wondering when we'd find time to get you to the camping grounds today. Grab your camera and come with me. It just wouldn't be a Ballochburn calendar without pictures of the campers.'

'It doesn't sound too serious,' she added a minute later as she held the back door of the Jeep open for Bella to jump inside. 'Someone's burned their hand in the kitchen. They've got it under running water so I told them I'd go there rather than having him brought to the hospital.'

She was still avoiding looking at him for more than a second, Jack realised with dismay. Here they were with the first opportunity they'd had to be alone since they'd parted in the middle of the night and Jill was cheerfully talking—non-stop—about anything but that.

Going on about the unique Christmas feel the camping grounds had. How families came back year after year because they loved it so much. How there were now people bringing their children who were using the caravans or camp sites their own grandparents had used.

Was she avoiding the topic because it was unwelcome?

Thank goodness he had managed to control himself last night. Not to try and take that kiss any further.

God knew, he had wanted to.

The taste and scent of this woman. The first touch of his lips on hers and he had plunged into another time and space. A place of unimaginable excitement. Pleasure. Sheer....*warmth*.

A place of total acceptance. Even after he'd confessed his dreadful, dark secret, Jill hadn't rejected him.

She had, instead, given him the answer he'd been seeking.

It was simple, really, wasn't it?

In the emotional bank, his account was overdrawn and in order to top it up, all he needed was someone to give him the funds. Or rather, someone he could earn the funds from because he wasn't a charity case.

Jill was the most giving person he'd ever met. She just gave to everybody, no questions asked. She didn't seem to ask anything in return but she clearly received as much as she needed for her own account to stay firmly in the black.

She would give to Jack if he asked, but he wasn't going to ask. Not unless he had something of equal value that he could give in return. And maybe Jill didn't want anything more from him. Maybe that was why she was avoiding the topic—and any significant eye contact.

Jack let Jill's chatter wash over him, making noncommittal but encouraging noises when required. Trying to pick up any signals, verbal or otherwise, that Jill might want to talk about something more personal.

Like that kiss.

Hadn't she said they were allowed a little bit of Christmas magic?

That was before she knew you were a doctor, Jack reminded himself. Before she knew that you'd lied to her. Or how emotionally bankrupt you are.

It wasn't a very long journey to the camping grounds down in the valley beside the river.

Not nearly long enough to convince himself that he had anything worth offering Jill.

The manager of the camping ground met the Jeep and directed Jill towards a concrete block building that housed the showers at one end and the kitchens at the other.

'Is it OK if Jack, here, wanders round to get some photos?'

'Sure. Is this for the calendar I was hearing about in the pub last night?'

'Yes.' Jack nodded at the man. 'I hear it wouldn't be complete without having the camping ground in it.'

'Too right, it wouldn't. Feel free, mate.'

Jack wandered around as Jill disappeared into the kitchens. He hadn't expected such a Christmas feel to a makeshift settlement of tents and caravans so he was astonished at what he found.

Tents that had decorations tied to their poles. Caravans decked out in coloured lights. People wearing Christmas hats and umpteen over-excited children. Some were already in the river, trying out new inflatable toys and a canoe or two. One was trying to Rollerblade on grass and several teenage girls were sitting together, madly texting on shiny new mobile phones.

The way Jarred would be before too long.

The image of the look on the boy's face that morning would stay with Jack for ever. The gift had meant so much. Not the phone—that had been just the bit that could be wrapped. They had both known what the real gift was. Support. Having someone in the world that cared about you.

He could give *that* to Jill.

Hell, he could give her all the love that had been bottled up inside him all his life.

He could share her laughter.

Hold her when she needed to cry.

Make sure her account was overflowing even if she was a world away from this magical place she'd grown up in.

Jack's step felt almost urgent as he made his way to the camp kitchens. Jill was still in there and things couldn't be too serious, judging by the laughter and loud, cheerful voices.

Several families were using the facilities to prepare their Christmas dinners by the look of it. Women with champagne glasses nearby were making salads. Men held cans of beer and poked at basins full of marinating meat.

'Pete'll do anything to get out of the cooking,' one was shouting.

'Nah.' Someone else laughed. 'He *was* doing the cooking. He got his fingers mixed up with the sausages.'

'Yeah—easy mistake!'

Jill was using damp teatowels to wrap the man's scorched-looking palm. 'We'll keep it cool until we can get you to the surgery and put a proper burn dressing on it.' She spotted Jack. 'First-degree burn,' she told him. 'Painful but not serious. Anyone want to come with Pete and give him a ride back here?'

'Nah.' A man lifted a beer can in salute. 'Walk'll do you good, mate!'

'That's my beer you're drinking, Wayne!'

'So it is! Guess I better come along and be the taxi, then.'

'Pete can ride with me,' Jill said. 'Could you take Jack? We're a bit short on seats in the Jeep.'

No chance to talk to Jill about anything personal on the way back to the hospital, then, and goodness knew what kind of chaos was brewing for the rest of the day. Jack could have been disheartened. Probably would have been except that Jill looked at him. Caught his gaze properly for the first time that day. And she smiled at him.

That warm, loving kind of smile she was so good at.

Just for him.

Jack followed Wayne to his car with a seed of hope taking root. Blossoming even.

It didn't need to be ruthlessly weeded out, the way nine-year-old Jack had learned to do in order to save the disappointment at seeing it wither and die before it could bear fruit.

No. This was it.

Fate had dropped him from the sky because the answer had been waiting for him, right here in the heart of stone-fruit country.

And he had found it.

* * *

It didn't take long to sort out a suitable dressing for Pete's hand and supply some pain relief.

'You'll need to keep it dry,' Jill warned. 'And I want to see it again tomorrow.'

'Won't be able to wash the dishes after dinner, then.' Pete grinned. 'Shame!'

'He won't need those pills,' Wayne joked. 'A few tinnies should anaesthetise that hand pretty well.'

'Go easy.' Jill smiled. 'And have a good rest of Christmas.'

'You, too,' the men chorused.

'We won't,' Jill informed Jack, 'unless we go and do our bit in the kitchen. Aunty Faith might provide all the food and the tablecloths and silverware and so on, but there's a lot to do to make it as perfect as she expects. I'll bet those peas are still waiting to get shelled.'

They were. It was nearly midday and Christmas dinner was due to be on the table at 2 p.m.

Not that the youngest patients in Ballochburn Hospital were expected to wait that long. Maisie had roasted a chicken for them.

'We'll say it's a small turkey,' she said, as she set the trays. 'Jarred can eat with the rest of us. He's not infectious any more and he's old enough for grown-up food.'

The grown-up turkeys had been in the ovens for hours now. A huge glazed ham sat waiting on a silver platter. Brussels sprouts filled a vast stainless-steel pan and a row of plum puddings sat like decorations on a side bench. Hope was making cranberry sauce. Wally was peeling a huge mound of potatoes, his Santa hat still in place, though slightly skew. He was delighted to see Jack.

'Grab a peeler, lad, and come and tell me all about that plane of yours. Latest model Cessna, isn't it?'

'Yep. A Skyhawk SP.'

'Wouldn't mind taking it for a bit of a spin.'

'You'd be very welcome, as soon as it's airworthy again.'

'Won't be long, lad. The parts turned up on the bus last night. I'll get onto it first thing in the morning. Civil Aviation still has to do their little investigation bit but I'm sure that won't be a problem. You'll be up and away in no time.'

Up.

And away.

Jill stopped eating the peas she was shelling and started putting them in the pot like she was supposed to.

Would Jack come back when he had found the answers he needed?

Would she still be here?

She had to find a way of trying to let him know that she would welcome him back into her life if he chose to come. Whenever that might be and wherever she was. He would be able to find her whereabouts by asking someone in Ballochburn. Her family would always be here.

Jill looked at her mother's back as she stood stirring the sauce and then at her father, busy sharpening a wicked-looking carving knife by swiping it on a steel. She didn't realise she had sighed aloud until she felt her great-aunt's gaze.

'I hope you're not eating too many of those peas, Jillian.' Faith picked up a stack of linen napkins and silver serviette holders. 'I'm just going to help finish setting the tables,' she said. 'I'll send Judith Cartwright down for the crackers and then—'

Whatever was next on Faith's agenda remained unknown. The clatter of the heavy steel dropping on the tiled floor made everybody jump.

'Jim!' The colour drained from Hope's face. 'Whatever is wrong?'

Peas fell from Jill's suddenly numb fingers. Her father's face was a dreadful shade of grey with an unnatural shine of perspiration. He had a fist pressed to the centre of his chest—the classic sign of someone suffering from unbearable chest pain.

This was no simple angina attack. GTN and oxygen were not nearly enough to combat the pain.

'He's having an infarct, isn't he?'

Thank goodness Jack was here. He and Wally carried Jim through to the surgery. Even if Jill's hand hadn't been injured, she would have had difficulty attaching the ECG electrodes. Or drawing up the morphine he needed.

This was her *father*.

And he could be dying.

'Looks like an inferior.' Jack added the pink twelve-lead ECG trace to the folder of notes. 'How far away is that helicopter?'

'Shouldn't be long now.'

Hope hadn't left her husband's side since he'd collapsed in the kitchen. She was still clutching his hand.

'Don't you dare die on me, Jim Metcalf!'

'I thought you were sick of me.'

'How could I be sick of you? I don't see you often enough to get sick of you, you silly man. How many times have I told you you work too hard?'

'Not hard enough,' Jim mumbled. 'I should have been around to help you more.'

'I don't need help,' Hope sniffed. 'All I needed was to get noticed sometimes.'

Faith didn't need to come into the surgery to tell them the rescue helicopter had been spotted. They could all hear the welcome sound of the approaching transport that would hopefully get Jim to emergency care and treatment before too much of his heart muscle was damaged.

'I'm coming with you,' Hope declared.

'Of course you are,' Jim agreed. 'Wouldn't be able to live without you, Hope. Wouldn't want to.'

'I'm coming, too.' Jill smiled at her mother and handed her some tissues.

'You can't,' Jim said. 'We can't leave Ballochburn without a doctor.'

'What's wrong with Mr Sinclair, then?' Faith queried. 'Or Dr Sinclair, so I've been told. ' She eyed the syringe Jack was holding as he prepared to top up Jim's level of pain relief. 'He certainly *seems* to be living up to his new reputation.'

Jill had seen that kind of fear in Jack's eyes before this. When she had offered to give him some Christmas magic. He wasn't ready to have that much asked of him. It could be as much of a disaster as Jill asking for some kind of commitment before he'd had a chance to get to know her. And trust her.

'I'll stay,' she said quietly.

The relief on Jack's face didn't last long, however. It barely registered before the door of the surgery flew open.

'Help! Someone, *help*!'

Maisie had a small limp body cradled in her arms.

'It's Nat,' she cried desperately. 'He's *choking*!'

CHAPTER ELEVEN

THE roar of the rescue helicopter landing in the car parking area directly outside the surgery was deafening.

Nobody inside the room took the slightest notice.

Jack had taken Nat from Maisie's arms. 'What happened?'

'He was eating chicken off Mel's plate…' Tears streamed down Maisie's fat red cheeks. 'He was really hungry, poor wee lamb. He stuffed it in and…and then he stopped breathing…'

Jack was sitting down in the chair beside the desk as Maisie sobbed out the history. He tipped the toddler face down over his knees, supporting his head with one hand. With the heel of his other hand, he delivered rapid and forceful blows between Nat's shoulder blades.

Then he turned the child face up, keeping his head lower than his chest. Jill could see the awful blue tinge to the lips. There was no sound or sign of any air movement. There was complete airway obstruction and Nat was clearly unconscious.

'Try chest thrusts.' Woozy from the morphine and his voice muffled by the oxygen mask, Jim was struggling to sit up on the bed. Hope clung to his arm, trying to keep him from getting up.

'Stay where you are, Dad.' Jill pulled a laryngoscope from its case on a shelf and snapped the blade open to turn on the light.

'Can you open his mouth?' she asked Jack. 'I'll see if anything's visible.'

Something was. Lodged too far back in the toddler's mouth to reach with fingers, and Jill wasn't about to try. She could end up pushing it further down and causing more damage.

'Where are your Magill forceps?' she asked her father.

'With the bag mask…side pocket of the life pack.'

'There's no time,' Jack snapped. 'He's blue.' He bent down, placing his mouth over Nat's, holding his nose shut and trying to push air in with mouth-to-mouth ventilation.

'I'm barely getting anything in,' he said grimly, seconds later.

At that moment the still open doorway to the surgery was filled by new arrivals.

Two paramedics and behind them Faith and Jarred.

'What the hell's going on?' a paramedic queried. 'I thought we were coming for a cardiac patient.'

'This kid's choking,' Jack informed them tersely. 'You qualified to do a needle cricothyroidotomy?'

'Yes, but the kit's still in the chopper.'

'It won't be enough,' Jill said urgently. Creating an airway with a wide-bore needle was a temporary solution. Even if they could remove the obstruction in the time they bought, the likelihood of swelling and repeat closure of the airway meant that a longer-term solution was vital. 'He needs a surgical airway,' she added decisively.

'Get on with it, then,' Jack said. 'We're losing too much time.' He tried to deliver another breath to Nat.

'I can't, Jack!' Jill held up her right hand with the strapping on the two middle fingers. 'You'll have to do it.'

* * *

Time seemed to freeze.

Jill could see the enormity of what she was asking Jack to do.

To face his worst nightmare.

To revisit the appalling incident that had driven him away from practising medicine.

To take full responsibility for trying to save a child's life.

She could feel her eyes filling with tears as she crouched beside the man on the chair, still holding the unconscious child. She laid her hands over his.

'Jack,' she whispered. 'You can do this. *Please.* Do it for Nat. For me…for *yourself.*'

Then the frozen moment was gone and all hell broke loose.

A paramedic ran for gear. Jack laid Nat on the floor. Jill scrambled to find what they needed.

Jim could only watch from his bed, with Hope's arms around him.

Faith had her arms around Jarred.

'It'll be all right,' Jill heard her say over and over again, like a mantra. 'It'll be all right.'

Jack had never felt anything like this.

Such sheer panic.

Holding the utterly limp child in his arms. Looking up to see Jarred's gaze fixed on him from the corner of the room the boy was wedged into.

Do something, he seemed to be yelling silently. You've got to *do* something.

Feeling Jill's hands gripping his. The transfer of warmth.

Strength.

Hearing her voice. The belief that rang through in her words.

He *could* do this.

He *had* to.

For Nat. For Jarred. For himself. But perhaps most of all for Jill because she believed in him. Because she touched his soul in a way no one had ever touched him.

He would do anything she ever asked of him.

Even take a scalpel to a tiny child's throat. Cut into it. Reverse his hold and insert the handle of the scalpel into the incision and rotate it to open the airway.

It was Jill who held out the smallest-size endotracheal tube to be inserted and a paramedic who had the suction equipment ready. It was Jack who connected the bag-valve device and secured the tube with fingers that still weren't trembling. He attached the bag mask and gave Nat his first full lungs of oxygen in what seemed like far too many minutes.

And it was Jack who took the Magill forceps now that they had time and opened Nat's mouth. He held the tongue out of the way with the blade of the laryngoscope and shone the light on the obstruction.

It was a sharp piece of bone hiding inside the chicken meat. Jack had to work very carefully to ease it out without doing any further damage. He held it up a minute later, still gripped in the forceps, for everybody to see.

'You got it!' Jim sank back onto his pillows, closing his eyes in relief.

'He's breathing for himself,' Jill cried. 'Look!'

Seeing the small chest rise and fall without the assistance of the paramedic holding the bag mask was a joy, but Jack wasn't going to let himself relax just yet. Even when the monitor clipped onto Nat's tiny finger revealed that the oxygen saturation was up to one hundred per cent.

'There could be a lot of swelling from that obstruction. I can't see how much damage there is. He's going to need the airway for a while.'

He needed rapid transport as well. Intensive monitoring with surgical back-up if necessary. Expert assessment and enough time to gauge whether his brain had been deprived of oxygen long enough to sustain permanent damage.

Or maybe the time needed would not be as long as Jack feared.

Nat was stirring. Regaining consciousness. His eyes opened and he gazed in dismay at the strange and frightening environment he found himself in. His face crumpled as he began to cry soundlessly. His gaze roved, seeking a more familiar face than the medics still crouched over him.

Jim gave Hope a gentle push. 'He needs you, love.'

'So do you.' Hope was clearly reluctant to let go of her husband. 'He knows Maisie as well as me.'

'It's OK,' Jim murmured drowsily. 'As long as I know you're close. They need you as much as I do, my love. All those children have. For years.'

So Hope crouched on the floor and cuddled Nat as best she could while preparations around them gathered momentum.

'Jack had better go with you,' Jill said. 'To keep an eye on Nat.'

'That'll still leave Ballochburn without an able-handed doctor,' Faith pointed out. 'What if something else happens?'

'But Nat needs a medical escort. So does Dad, for that matter.'

'So what's wrong with these paramedics?' Faith asked bluntly. 'Don't they train these people to manage situations like this?'

'Indeed they do, ma'am.' The paramedics exchanged amused glances. 'I think we can safely transport both our patients here. We're running a bit short of space in the chopper as it is—unless Mrs Metcalf wants to stay behind?'

'No,' said Hope.

'No,' said Jim.

Nat's little fists closed on the fabric of Hope's clothing as a silent testimony to his own wishes.

'I guess that settles it.' A paramedic nodded.

'Of course it does,' Faith said crisply. 'We need Jack *and* Jill here. They're a perfect team.'

Within minutes, everything was organised. Jim was loaded into the helicopter, his pain relief topped up, oxygen on and continuous ECG monitoring in place.

Nat was loaded as well, to travel in Hope's arms, also with oxygen on, although his oxygen saturation and his colour were perfectly normal.

All those left behind watched the helicopter take off and Jill was grateful for the firm grip with which Jack was holding her good hand.

'We'll give it a couple of hours,' Jack said. 'If we haven't heard from your mum by then, we'll ring the hospital and find out what's happening.'

How on earth was she going to get through this dreadful period of waiting?

Hearing Maisie sobbing behind her wasn't helping.

Faith appeared to agree.

'This is not your fault, Maisie Drummond, and that little lad is going to be fine. Our Dr Sinclair saved his life.'

Our Dr Sinclair. Miraculously, Jill felt a smile tugging at her lips. She looked up and caught Jack's gaze.

Her Dr Sinclair. She held his hand more tightly.

'We've got a ward full of people waiting for their Christmas dinner, Maisie,' Faith said sternly. 'I think the plum puddings could spare a little of their brandy and when we've fortified ourselves, we'll get on with doing what needs to be done.'

Maisie rallied and sniffed bravely.

Jill squeezed Jack's hand again as Faith led Maisie away.

'You did it, Jack,' she said quietly. 'You *did* save Nat's life. I'm so proud of you.'

I love you, she wanted to say. But maybe she didn't need to. The way Jack was looking at her right now made her feel as though she had already said the words.

That he'd said them right back to her.

'You believed in me,' Jack said softly. 'You have no idea how much that means.'

'Oh, I think I do.'

'And Jarred—did you see the look on his face?'

'No.' Jill turned to where Faith and Maisie had almost reached the door. 'Where *is* Jarred?'

'Oh, Lord!' Faith turned back, completely losing her customary air of calm assurance. 'He ran away when Jack was about to put that tube into Nat's neck. With everything else happening, I clean forgot to go looking for him.'

'We'll find him,' Jack said.

Faith looked at the way he was still holding Jill's hand. At how closely together the two of them were standing. Her face relaxed noticeably and she nodded.

'Bring him back in time for dinner,' she instructed. 'And, Jack?'

'Yes?'

'We'll need you to carve the turkey, seeing as James isn't here.'

The children's room was quiet.

Elise lay on her bed with Carol sound asleep beside her in the plastic crib borrowed from the maternity ward. Cuddled under each arm she had Jade and Mel. Now worn out from a morning's excitement, they lay listening to Elise read them one of their new story books.

Angela was watching over them all. She went pale on seeing Jack and Jill enter the room. She opened her mouth but clearly couldn't bring herself to utter the question on her lips.

'Nat's fine,' Jack said.

'Where is he?' Jade's halo was still on but her wings were crumpled as she lay on her side, close to Elise.

'He had to go to the hospital,' Jill told her. 'He needs special looking after, just for a day or two, and then he'll come back.'

'We saw the helicopter,' Mel said. ' Where's Jarred?'

'That's what we wanted to ask you.' Jill caught Jack's gaze but had to look away quickly. He cared as much as she did for the welfare of the oldest of these children. He was just as worried. 'You haven't seen him, then?'

'Not since Nat went away.'

They did a quick search of the rest of the hospital, including the kitchens. The ovens had been turned well down and Faith and Maisie sat at the table. Wally was topping up their brandy glasses.

'It's been a shock,' he was saying. 'Everyone will understand if dinner is a little later than usual.'

Maisie spotted Jill. 'There's been a phone call,' she said importantly.

'From Dunedin?' Jill caught her breath. 'Are they at the hospital already? Why didn't Mum call me on my mobile?'

Maisie flapped her hand at Jill. 'Don't interrupt, Jilly Metcalf. Where are your manners? No. The call was from that woman from Invercargill. Margaret somebody.'

'The social worker?'

'That's the one.' Maisie took another fortifying sip of brandy.

'What did she say?'

'She said to wish you all a Merry Christmas.'

'Oh…' It wasn't very merry, was it? So far, it was shaping up to be the most disastrous Christmas Day Jill had ever experienced.

'She also said they've got hold of the grandparents. In London they were, but they're rushing home to collect the children. Should be here in a day or two.'

'That's good.' But Jill couldn't help sounding dubious. They had to find Jarred. Had to reassure themselves that Nat was really on the way to a full recovery. These children needed reuniting and then settling before another major change was forced upon them.

'It's very good,' Faith said firmly. 'They need their family. It sounds as though these grandparents have been trying to help for a long time but their daughter refused to let them. Could be the best thing that could happen for them all.'

'Maybe he went to find Bella,' Jack suggested as they left the kitchen a short time later. 'He really loves that dog.'

They went to the gardener's shed but there was no sign of a boy or a dog.

They searched the gardens.

'Hey!' Jill stopped suddenly. 'What's your cellphone number, Jack?'

He told her. Jill pulled her own mobile from her pocket and began texting.

Jarred? Jill here. Where R U?

'He may not have it with him,' Jack warned.

'I saw the way he was looking at you when you gave it to him,' Jill responded. 'I don't think he'll be putting it down in a hurry.'

Sure enough, her phone beeped.

Lukin 4 Bela was the response.

Where? Jill sent back.

Hens came a succinct reply.

'I know where he is,' Jill said in relief. 'Come with me.'

She led Jack rapidly along the track beneath the old oak trees, through the squeaky gate and into the back garden of her childhood home.

And there, on the swing beneath the apple trees, was Jarred. His head down, his feet scuffing dusty earth. Spotted hens hovered nearby, keeping an eye on the newly disturbed dirt in case any edible treasure was uncovered.

'I can't find her,' Jarred said. 'She's gone.'

'She won't have gone far,' Jill said hopefully. 'We'll find her.'

Jarred wouldn't look up. 'Nat's dead, isn't he? Just like Mum.'

'No.' Jack squatted in front of the swing. 'He's not dead, Jarred.'

'I saw what you did.' Jarred sounded disgusted. 'You made him bleed.'

'I had to, mate. He couldn't breathe. I had to make a little hole and put a special tube into his neck so he could breathe. So he *wouldn't* die. He's OK, now, honest.'

'Why did they put him in the helicopter, then? And take him away?'

'Because they need to watch him for a while and then take the tube out and fix up the little hole. When they're sure it's safe to do that.'

Jarred finally looked up. A brief, hurt glance. 'I thought you were trying to kill him.'

Jill almost groaned aloud. It hadn't just been Jack's worst nightmare, had it?

'Oh, mate…' Jack's words were a soft groan. 'That is the last thing on earth I would ever try to do. You didn't *really* think that, did you?'

The eye contact was held longer this time. 'I guess not,' Jarred admitted. 'I…was scared.'

'Want to know a secret?' Jack asked.

'OK.'

'I was scared, too.'

'But you still did it.'

'Yeah. Sometimes you have to do things that scare you.' Jack rose to his feet again. 'Sometimes, if you're really lucky, you can find someone that helps you do the scary things and then they're not so scary.'

He was looking at Jill. Smiling.

She smiled back, loving the way he was looking at her. As though she was the most important person on earth. As though he didn't want to look anywhere else for as long as possible.

'So where's Bella, then?' Jarred asked. 'Why did she run away?'

'I don't know,' Jill said. 'But she's been sleeping on the

veranda. I put a nice woolly blanket there for her. Shall we go and see if she's having a nap or something?'

'OK.'

Jarred climbed wearily off the swing, the weight of the world resting on him again. Jack put a hand on his shoulder.

'How well do you know your grandparents, mate?'

'Nanna and Pop? We don't get to see them much. They live in the country up near Dunedin somewhere.'

'Are they nice?' Jill asked carefully.

'Yeah.'

'They're worried about you guys.' Jack also sounded a little wary. 'They're on their way home so they can come and look after you all.'

Jarred's shoulders hunched. 'I don't want them to look after us. I want to stay here.'

'You could always come and have holidays here,' Jill offered. She knew her mother would say the same thing if she had been here and seen how sad this little boy was.

Jarred looked up at Jill. 'Will you be here?'

'Um…I do have to go away.' Jill could feel Jack watching her. She couldn't look back. Couldn't let him see how hard it was going to be for her to leave. 'I'll be coming back for holidays, too, though.'

'Why do you have to go away?'

'Because I need to do my job. I need to be a doctor.'

'But isn't that what you're doing here?'

'Um…yes…' Jill's step slowed so that she was behind the others as they climbed the veranda steps.

It was exactly what she was doing here. Looking after inpatients like Betty and old Mrs Hinkley and the chickenpox children. Accidents like Nick and the cherry picker and Jack after his plane crash. House visits like the one to Sue and Emma.

She needed to go back there later today. To help with arrangements and offer support.

The kind of support that would be needed for a long time. The kind that built the bonds that could hold friends and even a whole community together.

Jarred turned to Jack at the top of the steps. 'You're a doctor, too, aren't you?'

'Yes, mate. I am.'

Jill caught her breath. He hadn't said he used to be a doctor but wasn't any more.

How could he say that after today? After caring for her father and saving Nat's life?

'So you have to go away, too?'

'Maybe.'

Maybe? Jill had to consciously release her breath. What did he mean, maybe? Was he thinking of *staying*?

In which case, what the hell was she thinking of going away for?

'I might stay for a while,' Jack continued calmly. 'Jill's dad needs some help around here and Jill's got a sore hand. That is...' he turned to catch Jill's astonished gaze '...if that would be OK?'

It would be a lot more than OK.

'That would be great,' Jill managed. 'Really great.'

'Hey!' Jarred ran to the end of the veranda and dropped to his knees. 'Bella *is* here! But what's *that*?'

It was a puppy. The first of four.

All three of them hunkered down beside the dog, watching

the miracle of the births. Jack had one arm around Jarred's shoulders. His other hand caught Jill's and held it.

'Wish I had my camera,' he muttered.

They stayed that way for a long time, until the last puppy had been born and cleaned up and then nudged towards the others, who were having their first drink of milk. Bella looked up at her audience and her tail thumped gently.

'You're a clever, clever girl,' Jill told her.

'Can I have a puppy?' Jarred begged. 'Please? A dog of my very own?'

'We'll have to talk to Nanna and Pop about that,' Jill said. 'But if they live in the country and they don't mind, it would be fine by me. It could be my Christmas present to you.'

They were all late for Christmas dinner but nobody seemed to mind. Jack carved the rather dry turkey but Jill couldn't eat a bite. Not until the call came to say that Jim had been taken to the catheter laboratory and had undergone angioplasty with all the lesions on his coronary arteries successfully stented with complete resolution of his symptoms.

Suddenly there a lot more than just Christmas to celebrate.

'He'll have to take things easy for a while,' Faith declared. 'It's high time that man retired.'

'Look who's talking,' Wally boomed. 'When are *you* going to retire, Faith?'

'I hope I can help,' Jack said. 'I'm going to apply for the locum position here.'

Faith gave her great-niece a look that Jill couldn't interpret. 'Excellent,' the old lady said.

Another call came, when the plum puddings and the not very strong brandy sauce arrived at the table, to let them know that Nat was doing very well and that a procedure to repair his airway was booked for the next day.

All going well, both Jim and Nat would be coming home the day after that.

Wally, Judith and the other staff and members of the Friends of the Hospital committee went to their own homes and families after the tables were cleared and the dishes done. Faith went to have a lie down and Maisie took something for her headache and put her feet up with the new romance novel Jill had given her for Christmas.

'Just what the doctor ordered,' Maisie said contentedly. 'You lot can all go away and leave me in peace for a while.'

Jarred went to spend the rest of the afternoon sitting beside Bella, watching her feed her puppies.

Jill paid a visit to the Wheelers.

Jack went to print off some photographs and keep himself available in case anyone needing medical care turned up at Ballochburn Hospital.

There were no emergencies.

Except one.

The urgency had been building all afternoon but it wasn't until much later that Jill finally found a moment to be alone with Jack.

After an evening meal nobody had really wanted and all the inpatients had been checked and settled for the night.

The lights still twinkled on the ward tree. Jill could see them reflecting on the windows when she went into the garden at dusk to find Jack sitting on the bench. *His* bench.

She sat down beside him. And took his hand in hers.

'Merry Christmas, Jack.'

He smiled. Then the smile faded and he looked very, very serious. But not sad. That haunted look Jill had seen that first day had gone from his face. From those gorgeous dark eyes. He bent his head and kissed her. Softly.

'It's been the most amazing Christmas I've ever had,' he said. 'Thanks to you. And this place.' He kissed her again, his lips settling for just a little longer. Moving over hers as though exploring a place he felt incredibly lucky to be. 'Magic,' he murmured, drawing away.

'Do you really think you might stay?'

'I'd like to.' Jack reached out and touched Jill's face. Tracing its outline as he smiled. 'I've always hated Christmas. Dreaded it.' His fingers reached the bottom of her cheek and ran along her jaw. 'It's a time for home and family and celebrating all the things I've never had. Never thought I could have. But here…' His finger brushed Jill's lip, butterfly soft, as he released his breath in a quiet sigh. 'I feel like it's *been* Christmas. Like I'm…home. Does that make any sense?'

'Perfect sense.' Jill nodded. 'I love you, Jack.' The words just came out all by themselves.

'You hardly know me.'

'I know everything I need to know,' Jill said with conviction. 'You have a heart that's so caring it got broken because you cared too much and nobody cared enough about you.' She put her arms around Jack. '*I* care,' she whispered. 'I'm sorry I don't have a Christmas gift for you. All I can offer is that caring. My love.'

Jack's voice sounded curiously rough. As though tears were getting in the way. He took Jill into his arms.

'That's the biggest gift anyone could ever give.'

Jill's heart thumped painfully as she pulled away far enough to be able to see Jack's eyes. Will you accept it?' She tried to smile but her lips wobbled. 'It won't take much unwrapping.'

'Only if you accept the gift I have for you.' His gaze was holding hers—as gently as a caress.

Jill felt the world stop turning for an instant. 'You have a gift for me? What is it, Jack?'

'The only thing I have to give.' Jack had to clear his throat. 'Myself. My heart.'

It was too much. Joy threatened to tip into tears. Tears that could wash away all the worry and sadness that had been mixed into this extraordinary Christmas Day. Jill struggled to believe what she was hearing. That this wasn't way too good to be true.

'Does…your gift have a ribbon?'

'I'm afraid not.' Jack kissed her again. A kiss that was going to lead to a whole lot more. But passion needed to be held at bay for just a few moments more. Until Jill could really believe.

'Does it come with an exchange card?'

Jack laughed. A sound that chased away any doubts in Jill's mind. It was the sound of happiness.

'Definitely not.'

'Oh….' Jill could smile now and it only trembled a little bit. 'In that case, I accept.'

The exchange of their gifts was sealed in the only appropriate way as they kissed each other again. And then Jack stood up, picked Jill up in his arms and carried her beneath the old oak trees, through the squeaky gate, past where Bella lay with a snuggle of puppies and into her home.

Their home.

EPILOGUE

BALLOCHBURN'S fundraising calendar went on sale in October, in time for the following Christmas.

It didn't matter that most of the images were nearly a year old because they were timeless. They captured the spirit of a country community and a celebration that would never change.

They were also the record of a love story.

'I'm glad you put Bruce in first.' Jill was sitting on the top of the veranda steps of her old family home, with Jack beside her and Bella lying on the step just below their feet.

She loved the picture of the farmer in his black singlet and khaki hat, a long stalk of grass clamped between his teeth as he surveyed a paddock dotted with peacefully grazing sheep.

'It's the same paddock, isn't it? The one you crashed in.'

'I didn't crash, Jillian. It was a perfectly well-controlled forced landing.'

'Hmm.' Jill grinned as she twisted to touch the almost invisible scar on Jack's temple. Jack caught her hand and kissed the palm. Then he pulled her closer. He would have kissed her lips for a lot longer than Jill was clearly prepared to allow.

'I want to see the rest,' she excused herself. 'They look different now. All glossy and professional.'

'Mmm.' Jack sounded suitably modest. 'It's not a bad hobby to have, is it? I might keep it up.'

'You'd better. Aunty Faith is going to love this one of her house. She'll want to frame it.'

'Do you think she's finding it a bit crowded now, having your mum and dad living with her?'

'She loves it. And she does need an eye kept on her, even if she won't admit it.' Jill turned a page. 'I'm going to frame this one of Jarred and Bella. It's precious.'

'He loves that pup even more than Bella now. They're doing well in that obedience class, aren't they?'

'They're all doing well. They've got a wonderful home for the first time in their lives. We'll have to go and visit them again soon. Oh…' Jill turned another page. 'Pets' day!'

She laughed aloud at the image of Aaron Baker's legs in the air as a large black lamb made its bid for freedom.

Then she smiled fondly at the picture of Enid Hinkley's toothless grin as she draped tinsel on the Christmas tree.

'Shame she won't be here for this Christmas.'

'Mmm.' The sound was one of agreement but Jack's fingers stole unconsciously to the back of his thigh to give it a thoughtful rub.

Jill's head rested on Jack's shoulder as they flipped through the rest of the calendar.

A picture of the camping ground with a limp but well-decorated pine-tree branch attached to a tent pole—a group of laughing men toasting the photographer with their beer cans and children playing in the river in the background.

One of the carol service with the glow of candlelight on the rich red of the choir's robes.

One of small children in pyjamas with expressions of total

wonder on their faces as they gazed at a Santa who had a huge walrus moustache.

And the last picture.

'Do you think anyone will mind that we put in a wedding picture?'

'It's Christmassy,' Jack pointed out. 'Look at all those cherries on the trees behind us. And Sue's holding your bouquet—all red and white.'

'She's due any day now. Getting pregnant like that was so unexpected.'

'She hated the idea, didn't she?'

'Yes. She thought people would think she was trying to replace Emma.'

'Some things that get lost can never be replaced,' Jack said quietly. 'But I think it was meant to happen. A way of starting again for them.'

'Like us. We were meant to happen, weren't we?'

'Just like us.'

'Shall we tell anyone yet?'

Jack laid a gentle hand on Jill's belly. He smiled and shook his head.

'We've only just found out ourselves. Let's save the news. We could surprise everyone at Christmas dinner.'

'Another one of those gifts that can't be wrapped.'

'The best sort.' Jack wrapped his arms around his wife and held her close. 'Don't you think?'

'Absolutely.' Jill raised her face for a kiss, no less precious because it was now so familiar. 'The very best.'

MILLS & BOON®
MEDICAL™

Proudly presents

Brides of Penhally Bay

Featuring Dr Nick Tremayne

A pulse-raising collection of emotional, tempting romances and heart-warming stories – devoted doctors, single fathers, Mediterranean heroes, a Sheikh and his guarded heart, royal scandals and miracle babies…

Book One

CHRISTMAS EVE BABY
by Caroline Anderson

Starting 7th December 2007

A COLLECTION TO TREASURE FOREVER!
One book available every month

MILLS & BOON®
MEDICAL™

Proudly presents

Brides of Penhally Bay

*A pulse-raising collection of emotional,
tempting romances and heart-warming stories by
bestselling Mills & Boon Medical™ authors.*

January 2008
The Italian's New-Year Marriage Wish
by Sarah Morgan

Enjoy some much-needed winter warmth with
gorgeous Italian doctor Marcus Avanti.

February 2008
The Doctor's Bride By Sunrise
by Josie Metcalfe

Then join Adam and Maggie on a 24-hour rescue mission
where romance begins to blossom as the sun starts to set.

March 2008
The Surgeon's Fatherhood Surprise
by Jennifer Taylor

Single dad Jack Tremayne finds a mother for his
little boy – and a bride for himself.

*Let us whisk you away to an idyllic Cornish town –
a place where hearts are made whole*

COLLECT ALL 12 BOOKS!

FREE

4 BOOKS AND A SURPRISE GIFT!

We would like to take this opportunity to thank you for reading this Mills & Boon® book by offering you the chance to take FOUR more specially selected titles from the Medical™ series absolutely FREE! We're also making this offer to introduce you to the benefits of the Mills & Boon® Reader Service™—

- ★ **FREE home delivery**
- ★ **FREE gifts and competitions**
- ★ **FREE monthly Newsletter**
- ★ **Books available before they're in the shops**
- ★ **Exclusive Reader Service offers**

Accepting these FREE books and gift places you under no obligation to buy; you may cancel at any time, even after receiving your free shipment. Simply complete your details below and return the entire page to the address below. You don't even need a stamp!

YES! Please send me 4 free Medical books and a surprise gift. I understand that unless you hear from me, I will receive 6 superb new titles every month for just £2.89 each, postage and packing free. I am under no obligation to purchase any books and may cancel my subscription at any time. The free books and gift will be mine to keep in any case.

M7ZEE

Ms/Mrs/Miss/Mr...................Initials ....
BLOCK CAPITALS PLEASE

Surname ....

Address ....

....

....Postcode ....

Send this whole page to:
The Reader Service, FREEPOST CN81, Croydon, CR9 3WZ